"I'm glad we met, in spite of the strange circumstances."

"I'm glad, too." Maybe from the moment he'd first seen her in that video, he'd known he'd seek her out. Something in her called to him.

She tilted her head up and rose on her toes to bring her face closer to his in silent invitation—an invitation he wouldn't refuse. He'd been wanting to kiss her, hesitant only because of the tenuousness of their relationship. Her lips warmed beneath his, as soft and sensuous as he'd imagined they would be. He deepened the kiss.

A flash of light distracted him, and reluctantly he lifted his head to look around. He saw nothing but the array of news vans and reporters across the street, though he couldn't shake the sense that something had happened that he should have paid attention to.

Colorado Crime Scene

CINDI MYERS

First Published in Great Britain 2016
By Mills & Boon, an imprint of HarperCollins*Publishers*
1 London Bridge Street, London, SE1 9GF

Large Print edition 2016

© 2016 Cynthia Myers

ISBN: 978-0-263-06659-3

Our policy is to use papers that are natural, renewable and recyclable products and made from wood grown in sustainable forests. The logging and manufacturing processes conform to the legal environmental regulations of the country of origin.

Printed and bound in Great Britain
by CPI Antony Rowe, Chippenham, Wiltshire

Cindi Myers is an author of more than fifty novels. When she's not crafting new romance plots, she enjoys skiing, gardening, cooking, crafting and daydreaming. A lover of small-town life, she lives with her husband and two spoiled dogs in the Colorado mountains.

For Vicki L.

Chapter One

Luke Renfro never forgot a face. The blessing and the curse of this peculiar talent defined his days and haunted his nights. The faces of people he knew well and those he had merely passed on the street crowded his mind.

He sorted through this portrait gallery of strangers and friends as he studied the people who hurried past him on a warm, sunny morning on Denver's 16th Street Mall, searching for anyone familiar, while at the very back of his mind whispered the question that plagued him most: What if he'd overlooked the one person he most needed to find?

He shoved aside that familiar anxiety and reviewed the details of his assignment today: young Caucasian male, probably early to midtwenties, slight, athletic build, five-eight or five-nine. He'd been clean shaven in the surveillance photos Scotland Yard had forwarded from London, his brown hair cropped very short. But even if he'd grown out his beard or dyed his hair, Luke would recognize him. It was what he did. It was why the FBI had recruited him and others like him, copying an idea implemented by the Brits—to assemble a group of "super-recognizers" to look for known criminals and stop crime before it happened.

Also on the list of people he hoped to spot was a fortysomething man with a swarthy complexion and iron-gray curls, and a stocky Asian man with a shaved head and a scar beside one eye. If he spotted any of these people, he was to bring them into headquarters for questioning.

He crossed the street and strolled past a row

of restaurants starting to fill up with the early lunch crowd. A strong breeze made the banners strung overhead pop and snap. Welcome, Racers! declared one. Colorado Cycling Challenge! proclaimed another. The man Luke was searching for wouldn't miss the race, though Luke hoped to find him before he ever had a chance to attend.

A flash of honey-blond hair in his peripheral vision sent a jolt of recognition through him, a physical shock, like finding something important he hadn't even realized he'd lost. He whirled around in time to see the woman step onto one of the shuttle buses that ran up and down the length of the pedestrian mall. Heart pounding, he took off down the sidewalk after the bus, ignoring the annoyed looks from the hipster couple he jostled in his haste.

He hadn't expected to see her here today, though logically he shouldn't have been surprised. She'd been in some of those Scotland

Yard videos also, and the image of her heart-shaped face framed by a stylish short haircut, her wide hazel eyes staring into the camera from beneath a fringe of honey-colored bangs, had stayed with him, standing out from the sea of anonymous faces filed away in his memory.

She stepped off the shuttle four blocks down, in front of a chain drugstore, the breeze blowing her swept-aside bangs into her eyes. She stopped and brushed the stray locks off her face, allowing him time to take in her skinny jeans, athletic shoes, pale green tank top, and a scarf of mingled blue and green knotted at her throat. Then she started walking again, long, confident strides covering ground quickly. Staying back half a block, he followed her as she headed to a boutique hotel and entered the lobby. Luke hurried to catch up, weaving his way through a family unloading luggage at the front door and two men consulting a street map just inside the entrance.

Soft classical music filled the lobby, which was decorated in Victorian red velvet and gold brocade. Luke scanned the crowd of tourists and businessmen, but the woman wasn't among them. A check of the elevators showed both were stopped on upper floors. Had she opted for the stairs, or passed through to the hotel bar? He hesitated. Did he enter the bar and search for her, or return to the mall and his original quarry?

"Excuse me."

He turned and stared into the angry eyes of the woman he'd been following. Hazel eyes of mingled green and gold, fringed with gold lashes. Eyes that had disturbed his dreams, though in those fantasies, they'd been considerably friendlier than they were right now. "Who are you, and why are you following me?" she demanded.

"I don't know what you're talking about."

Bluffing was as important a skill for an agent as it was for a poker player.

"I'm not stupid. I saw you following me." She folded her arms under her breasts; he wondered if she was aware how that emphasized her cleavage. If he pointed this out, she'd no doubt add "sexist pig" to whatever other unflattering descriptions she'd ascribed to him. "I want to know why."

She was calling his bluff. Time to fold. But that would mean leaving and walking away, and he hadn't gone to all this trouble to do that. Maybe a better answer was to show her his cards—or at least some of them. He reached into his jacket and pulled out the folder with his credentials. "Special Agent Luke Renfro. FBI."

Her eyes widened, and some of the color left her cheeks. "What is this about?" The words came out as a whisper, and all her bravado vanished. In fact, she looked ready to faint, her breath coming in quick, shallow pants.

Her reaction—more fear and guilt than an innocent citizen ought to exhibit—had all his instincts sounding alarms, his senses on high alert. He touched her arm lightly, though he was prepared to hang on if she made a run for it. "Why don't we go into the bar and talk?" He nodded toward the hotel bar, which at this time of day was almost deserted.

"All right." She allowed him to usher her into the bar, to a red leatherette booth. The lighting was subdued, the music almost inaudible. Luke sat across from the blonde, and the waitress, who'd been seated at one end of the bar, hurried over to them. "I'll have a glass of iced tea," Luke told her. He looked to the woman across from him. "Would you like something stronger?"

"Just water." She pushed her hair back out of her eyes and settled her hands flat on the table in front of her. Her nails were short, polished a deep blue. She wore silver earrings that glinted in the bar light when she turned her head to look at him. Her hair, thick and shiny and sexy, curled around her ears and the nape of her neck.

It bothered him that this woman had stuck in his head when so many others didn't. Maybe that's why he'd followed her, to see if up close he could identify the reason he'd become so fixated on her. But maybe it wasn't simple attraction at work here. Maybe his cop instincts recognized some guilt in her he couldn't yet put into words. He didn't want to think of her as a suspect, but he had to if he was going to do his job correctly.

"Why is the FBI following me?" she asked, reminding him they were alone again.

"First, tell me your name, since you already know mine."

She hesitated, then said, "Morgan Westfield."

The name itself didn't set off any alarm bells. Though his photographic memory for faces didn't carry over to names or facts and figures, he'd learned the names of key suspects in his current investigation—at least, the names they knew. A series of terrorist bombings had rocked the cycling world in the past two years, with bombs killing and injuring racers and spectators alike at key races around the world. The Bureau hoped that by sending members of the team they'd code-named Search Team Seven to Denver they could prevent another attack. Was Morgan somehow involved and Luke hadn't realized it?

"You were following me and you don't know my name?" she asked. "I don't understand."

"You were at the Tour de France last month," he said. "And the Tour of Britain before that." But not at the Paris-Roubaix the year before. Or maybe she'd managed to stay out of range of the security cameras for that event.

"You've been following me all this time?"

Her voice rose, and anger returned the color to her cheeks.

He hadn't been following her, but maybe fate or instinct or blind luck had led him to her. The waitress brought their drinks and glanced at them curiously. "Will there be anything else?"

"No, thank you." He handed her a ten. "Keep the change."

She stuffed the bill into her apron and retreated to the bar once more. Morgan leaned over the table toward him. "Why is the FBI following me?" she demanded again, tension straining her face.

"I'm not following you," he said. "I'm actually looking for someone else. But I remembered you and was curious."

"You remembered me?" She sat back, frowning. "But we've never met."

"No. But I've studied surveillance videos of both races." And many others. "I remembered seeing your face."

"That's crazy," she said. She didn't seem as nervous now, but more annoyed, as she had been when she'd first challenged him in the lobby. "There were thousands of people at those races. Hundreds of thousands. Why would you remember me?"

"It's what I do. It's my job, actually. I'm paid to remember faces, and to recognize them when I see them again."

She took a long drink of water, her eyes never leaving his. "I'm not sure that explanation makes sense."

"You know how some people have photographic memories, right?"

"You mean they can read a phone book or encyclopedia and remember everything on the pages? I thought that was just something in movies."

"No, it's a real phenomenon. My brother is like that. Once he reads something, it's committed to memory." A familiar ache squeezed his chest at the mention of his twin brother. He'd give anything to know where Mark was now. To be assured he was safe.

"But it's different for you?" Morgan prompted.

He nodded. "With me, it works a little differently. I never forget a face. Not if I've spent even a few seconds focusing on it."

"I thought they had computers that could do that—scan video for familiar faces and stuff."

"Facial-recognition software can't compete with the human brain," he said. "After riots in London in 2011, Scotland Yard's team of super-recognizers identified 1200 suspects from video surveillance. Computer software identified only one person."

"So I shouldn't be flattered that you remembered me—it's just something you do."

"Some faces are more pleasant to remember than others." He smiled, but she continued to regard him with suspicion.

Fine. He needed to be more suspicious of her,

as well. "What were you doing at the races?" he asked.

"I'm a writer. I was covering the races for *Road Bike Magazine*."

"So you work for the magazine?"

"No, I'm a freelancer. I write for a lot of different publications, though my specialty is bicycle racing."

"Are you in Denver to cover the Colorado Cycling Challenge?"

"What if I am?"

And what if she was here to do more than write about the races? "I'm here for the race, too," he said. "We'll probably see each other again."

"I never saw you at those other races."

"I wasn't there." Before she could ask the obvious question, he said, "I saw you on surveillance video."

She closed her eyes. Maybe she was counting to ten before she went off on him. When she opened them again, her voice was calm but chilly. "Why don't we stop this game of twenty questions right now and you give me some straight answers. What is this about? Why were you looking at surveillance videos of me? Why were you following me just now?"

"You want the truth?"

"Of course I want the truth."

"I wasn't looking for you on those videos, but you stuck in my head. I remember a lot of people, but most of them don't make any strong impression on me. But you did. I wanted to meet you and try to figure out why." That was the truth in its simplest form. Basic attraction leads to impulsive action. His bosses would not approve.

"Seriously?" She stared at him.

He nodded. "You said you wanted the truth, and that's it."

"I can't decide if that's the worst pickup line

I ever heard, or the best." Some of the tension went out of her and she sat back, studying him.

"You have to give me points for originality," he said.

This coaxed the beginnings of a smile from her. She had full lips, highlighted with a pink gloss. He wondered what it would feel like kissing those lips, then he pushed the thought away.

"So how does this memory thing of yours work?" she asked. "Do you just automatically remember everyone you've ever seen?"

"I have to focus on them for a few seconds, but yes, after that I'll recognize them again." As a small child, he thought everyone related to the world that way. Once he'd learned a face, he never forgot it. He remembered not only that he'd seen a person before, but where and what they'd been doing. Most of the time, it wasn't a particularly useful talent, not like Mark's memory for facts and written information. That talent had allowed him to breeze through school. He'd earned his PhD in physics before his twenty-fifth birthday, while Luke had been only an average student.

Then the FBI had come calling and he'd found his niche, the one place where his particular skill could make a difference.

Two men entered the bar, dressed casually in jeans and T-shirts, engrossed in conversation. He'd seen the older one earlier on the street, buying coffee from a food cart. The other one was the wrong race for any of his suspects, though he filed the man's face away for future reference, as was his habit.

"You're doing it now, aren't you?" Morgan asked. "Memorizing people."

"It's my job," he repeated.

"Is that why you're here—to memorize people at the bike race?"

"Let's just say I'm here for work, and leave it at that."

But he knew before he said the words that

she wasn't the type to leave it. "You're looking for someone, aren't you? Someone else you saw on those surveillance videos." She went very still; he wondered if she was holding her breath, waiting for his answer.

"I really can't talk about my assignment with a civilian. It's confidential." Maybe he'd already said too much.

"But I'm free to make an educated guess. And since you are a federal agent, I'd guess that you're here because of the terrorist who's been targeting bike races."

"Let's just say that after the bombings in Paris and London, there's a big law enforcement presence at this race." But only one small group was there with his assignment—to look for people who had been present when the other bombings occurred and bring them in for questioning. Only a handful of people had shown up at both the races where bombs had detonated, all of them men. Which didn't mean others weren't involved. That Morgan wasn't involved.

"There was serious discussion about canceling this race," she said. "The organization was just getting back on its feet after the doping scandals of several years ago, and now some nut job is setting off bombs at some of the biggest races." She leaned toward him again, her voice low. "That's why you're here, isn't it? You're looking for the bomber. Do you know who he is?"

Was she asking the question as a journalist or out of idle curiosity—or because she had a more personal interest in the answer? "I can't say."

"Of course, you know who he is. You said before you were here searching for someone who wasn't me. You're looking for the bomber." She stared into his eyes, as if she could see into his head and decipher the image of the bomber there. "Why can't you tell me who it is? I attend a lot of these races. Maybe I can help you find him."

"Or maybe he's a friend of yours and you'll run right to him and tell him the FBI is looking for him."

She gasped. "You don't really think that, do you?"

"I don't know. I don't know anything about you but what you've told me."

She tried to look wounded, but mostly she looked afraid. Because he'd hit too close to the truth? "Why does it matter so much to you?" he asked.

She stood, bumping the table and sending water from her glass sloshing onto the surface. "I have to go," she said.

"What did I say to upset you?" He stood, but she had already brushed past him, hurrying out of the bar and into the lobby.

He started after her but stopped in the door of the bar. What would he do when he caught up to her? Clearly, she was done talking to him. And he had no reason to keep her, only a gnawing uneasiness that something wasn't right.

Moving cautiously, keeping objects and other people between himself and Morgan, he followed her across the lobby. She stopped in front of the elevators and pulled out her phone, punching in a number. The anxiety on her face increased as she listened for a few seconds, then ended the call. She hadn't said anything, and he had the impression whoever she'd been trying to reach hadn't answered.

Had she been calling the bomber to warn him? His stomach knotted with a mixture of anger and disappointment. He didn't want her to be guilty, but he couldn't discard all the evidence that told him something wasn't right.

The elevator doors slid open and she stepped inside. He moved from behind the pillar that had shielded him and her eyes met his. Beautiful eyes, filled with an aching sadness. The sense of loss hit him like a punch. He recognized that grief because he'd felt it himself. Who had she lost, and what had he done to cause her such fresh pain?

Chapter Two

Morgan choked back a sob as the elevator doors slid closed. She squeezed her eyes shut and hugged her arms tightly across her body, forcing the emotions back into the box she usually kept so tightly shut. By the time the elevator opened on the twelfth floor she felt more in control. She checked the hallway for signs of Agent Renfro. She wouldn't have put it past the man to run up twelve flights of stairs to catch her outside her room. But the carpeted hallway, which smelled of old cigarette smoke overlaid with the vanilla potpourri that stood in bowls on tables by the elevators, was empty.

Safely in her room, she pulled out her phone again and hit the button to redial Scott's number. She pressed the phone to her ear, listening to the mechanical buzz, then the click to his voice mail. His familiar voice, terse but cheerful, said, "Leave a message," then came the disconnect. The mailbox had been full for months, and he never answered her calls. But she never gave up hope that one day he would pick up. And sometimes she called just to hear his voice. Three cryptic words that helped her believe he was safe and all right, somewhere.

She sank onto the edge of the bed and stared at the still life of a bowl of fruit on the opposite wall, the colors blurring as she kept her unblinking eyes fixed on it. If only she could dull her emotions as easily. At first she'd been annoyed—and yes, a little intrigued—that the good-looking guy in the suit was following her. She was sure she'd never seen him before, but, unlike Agent Renfro, she didn't have a good memory for faces. When he'd flashed his FBI credentials, she'd been afraid she might faint right there.

She'd been terrified he'd approached her because of Scott. He was in some kind of trouble—big trouble, if the feds were involved. She'd almost said as much but had swallowed the words. Why give the agent a name if he didn't have it? Worse, why put Scott on his radar if she was mistaken and he was looking for someone else?

She'd let herself be a little flattered when Luke Renfro told her he remembered her and was interested in knowing her better. Clean shaven, with thick dark hair cut short and deep blue eyes, he was the kind of man who would make any woman look twice. Relief had filled her at the thought of innocent flirtation. The FBI agent was good-looking, and when she allowed herself to relax and feel it, she could admit to a certain sizzle in the air between them.

He was interesting, too, with his unusual talent for remembering people. It was like knowing someone who could do complicated math in his head, or someone who remembered the phone numbers of everyone he knew.

Except Luke's talent had a more sinister side. His talk of the bombings hadn't made her feel any easier. When he'd all but admitted he was looking for the bomber, she'd wondered again why he'd approached her. Maybe the line about wanting to meet her was just an excuse. Maybe he'd only been pretending not to know her name in order to see what she'd say. He could have stopped her because he knew about her connection to Scott and he wanted to see if she knew anything more.

As much as she told herself Scott would never do something so horrible, how could she really know? The man she loved wasn't the man he had been lately. He might be capable of anything, even something as terrible as this.

"Scott, where are you?" she whispered. "What have you gotten yourself into?"

LUKE RETURNED TO his surveillance of the mall, alert for any sign of Morgan, as well as his suspects. Was she mixed up in the bombings somehow, or was she just an unneeded distraction from the more important work he had to do?

Dusk descended like a gray curtain as he made his way to his hotel, down the mall from the one where Morgan was staying. Once in his room, he shed his jacket and tie, and telephoned his supervisor to give his report. "No sign of any of our suspects," he said. "But a lot of familiar racers, support people and fans are converging on the city. Maybe I'll have better luck at the kickoff banquet tomorrow night."

"Steadman thinks he saw one of our guys at the airport yesterday afternoon, but he lost him in the crowd." Special Agent in Charge Ted

Blessing had the smooth bass voice of a television preacher, and the no-nonsense demeanor of a man who was comfortable with wielding authority. "If Steadman is right, we've got to stop this guy before he makes his move."

"If Travis says he saw the guy, he saw him," Luke said. Though he had no doubt Blessing would go to the mat to support his team, the Special Agent in Charge had never bothered to hide his skepticism about the whole super-recognizer phenomena. "And if he's here, we'll find him."

"Unless he gets past us again. He's avoided detection so far. Which is one reason our analysts think he can't be acting alone."

"I thought they'd decided that he was a lone wolf. Has some group claimed responsibility for the other attacks?"

"No. But other intelligence has come in that points to a terrorist cell with links to each of the bombing locations. We've got people trying to track down a connection to Colorado right now. Plus, we finally have results from the tests on the explosives he used in the London bombing. Scotland Yard believes the bomber used military-grade C-4. Not impossible for a civilian to obtain, but not something you'd pick up at the local hardware store, either."

"Maybe some of the other suspects on our list are involved."

"Maybe. Anything else of interest I should know about?"

The image of Morgan's frightened face flashed into his mind, but he pushed it away. "Nothing yet," he said. He wasn't ready to offer her up for the Bureau's scrutiny. Not until he'd had time to try to discover her secret himself.

They said goodbye and ended the call and he retrieved his tablet from the room safe and booted it up. Time to do a little research into Morgan Westfield.

The knot in his stomach loosened a little as he read through the search engine results on her name. She'd been telling the truth about being a writer. Every hit featured one of her articles, mostly about cycling. He read through her recap of the Tour of Britain, caught up in her depiction of the excitement and tension of a sport he hadn't thought much about before being assigned to his case. The Bureau had briefed him and his fellow agents on the basics—how races are organized into stages, which could combine circuit races, cross-country treks and individual time trials. He understood the concept of racing teams that worked together to support one or more favorite riders, and had read about the dedication of the men for whom professional racing was their life.

But those facts hadn't breathed life into the events the way Morgan did in her article. Reading her words, he felt the struggle of the racers to meet the demands of the challenging course, the devotion of the fans who followed the peloton from stage to stage and the resources that went into putting on an event that was popular around the world.

He hesitated over the keys, then typed in another name, one he tried to refrain from searching but always came back to, month after month: Mark Renfro. The familiar links scrolled down the screen: an article Mark had written about the destructive potential of so-called dirty bombs, a piece for a scholarly journal on nuclear fission, a profile of him when he won a prestigious award from the University of Colorado, where he taught and conducted his research.

Farther down the page were articles about his disappearance almost a year before: Top Nuclear Physicist Missing. Professor Mark Renfro Missing, Feared Dead.

Luke read through that article, though he'd long ago memorized the text.

Mark Renfro, professor of nuclear physics at the University of Colorado in Boulder, has been reported missing after failing to return from a hiking trip in Colorado's remote Weminuche Wilderness area. Professor Renfro set out alone to hike to the top of Wilson Peak on Monday, and has not been seen since a pair of hikers reported passing him on the trail at about noon that day. Renfro was an experienced hiker who had reportedly been struggling with depression since the death of his wife in a car accident six months earlier. One colleague at the university, who wished to remain anonymous, stated he feared Renfro had arranged the hike with the intention of committing suicide.

Luke exited the screen, familiar anger rising up inside him. Mark had not committed suicide. Yes, he'd been devastated by Christy's death in the accident, but he would never have left their four-year-old daughter, Mindy, alone. Something had happened to keep him from coming back to the girl. Luke was certain his brother was still alive, and he would give anything to bring him back.

He'd driven Mark to the trailhead that day and arranged to meet him back there in two days. Luke's work schedule had prevented him from accompanying his brother on the hike, but Mark had taken these solo treks before. "I get some of my best ideas out there with no one else around," he'd said. Far from being depressed, he'd been in good spirits that morning. In the early hours, the sky showing the first faint hint of light, only one other car had been at the trailhead. Luke had scarcely glanced at the two dark figures inside. He wasn't working, and he didn't need to clutter his mind with more strangers' faces.

But what if he had taken the time to memorize those men? Were they the key to finding his brother and he'd missed his chance? He closed his eyes and tried again to picture the scene, but his mind came up blank. All he saw was Mark's face, smiling, eager to set out. Not the face of a man who was walking to his death.

THE NEXT MORNING, aided by a sleeping pill and a half hour of yoga, Morgan was feeling calmer. She headed down to the hotel's free breakfast buffet, her mind on her plans for the day. In addition to writing several articles for *Road Bike Magazine*, she'd been hired to blog about each day's race stage for the popular *Cycling Pro* website. Today she had an interview with an Italian rider who was one of the top contenders to win the race, then a Skype meeting with one of the UCI officials to get his views on the race. The Union Cycliste Internationale oversaw every aspect of sanctioned modern bicycle road races. In the wake of the bombings that had rocked other races, they had a lot riding on the success of this Colorado event.

Thoughts of the bombings brought her back to Agent Luke Renfro. He obviously knew more about the attacks than he was telling her. Maybe she needed to find him and pump him for more information. He'd said he was going to be around for the race. Maybe she'd spot him tonight, at the banquet to kick off the race festivities, before the racers headed out to the starting point in Aspen tomorrow. Under the guise of making small talk, she could question him, and maybe get a better feel for whether or not he was as dangerous to her peace of mind as he'd felt last night.

She found a table at the back of the breakfast room and was slathering strawberry jam onto a piece of wheat toast when Luke Renfro pulled out the chair across from her and sat down.

Her initial pleasure at seeing him again quickly gave way to nervousness. Her heart fluttered and she had to set aside the knife before she dropped it. "What are you doing here?" she asked, avoiding meeting his gaze.

He was dressed more casually today, in a blue pinstriped oxford shirt open at the collar, the sleeves rolled up to reveal tanned forearms lightly dusted with brown hair. He smelled of shaving cream—a clean, masculine scent that made her stomach flutter in rhythm with her racing heart.

"I had some more questions for you." He unfolded a napkin across his lap, then picked up the mug of coffee he'd brought with him.

"You won't tell me anything, so why should I share anything with you?"

"After I got back to the hotel last night, I went online and read some of your work. You're very good. I'm curious why you're a freelancer, and not on staff with one of the top cycling publications."

She told herself it wasn't creepy that he'd looked her up online. Everyone did it these days, whether they were checking out potential job applicants or prospective dates. So why did it make her so nervous that this particular man had been checking out her background? "Those staff jobs aren't necessarily easy to come by," she said. She sipped her coffee, her hands steady enough to drink it without spilling. "Anyway, I prefer the flexibility of freelancing."

"I didn't mean to upset you yesterday," he said. "What, exactly, did I say that made you so afraid?"

"I wasn't afraid." Her voice squeaked on the last word and she looked away.

"You may be an excellent writer, but you're a lousy liar."

When she dared to look at him again he was smiling. His lack of hostility soothed her a little, and in that moment she made a decision. She pulled out her phone and thumbed to the picture library. She turned the screen toward him. "Is this the man you're looking for?" Her voice quavered, and her heart pounded painfully, drowning out the clatter of cutlery and chatter of the diners around them.

She'd taken the photograph of Scott almost a year ago, on a hike in the Texas hill country, near their home in Austin. He stood with his slender frame leaning against a bent pine tree, a breeze blowing his blond hair across his face. He'd refused to smile for the camera or even to look directly at her. At the time, she'd thought he was merely being stubborn and moody; now she recognized the first signs that he wasn't himself, that what he always referred to as "his demons" were getting the best of him.

"Who is this?" Agent Renfro asked, his expression giving away nothing.

"First, tell me if he's your bombing suspect." Even saying the words made her feel a little faint, but better to know the truth than to keep wondering.

"No."

Relief flooded her, leaving her weak and shaky. She set aside the phone and sagged back against the chair. "Thank God," she whispered, not even caring that he saw her so undone.

"But I've seen him before," he said, his smile gone, his voice serious.

"Where?" she demanded. "When?" *Was he all right? Was he safe? Was he in trouble?*

"First, tell me who he is. And who he is to you."

"He's my brother. My older brother. Scott."

Something—surprise?—flickered in Luke's eyes. Followed by sympathy. He definitely didn't look as threatening. "He was in London," he said. "At the Tour of Britain."

"Oh." She put her fingers to her lips, too late to hold back the cry. To think that she'd been so close to him but hadn't seen him.

"You're looking for him, aren't you?" Luke's voice was gentle, his blue eyes full of understanding. "That's why you freelance—so you can travel around and look for him."

"Yes." She swallowed, reining in her emotions. "He disappeared ten months ago. But before that, he was a bicycle racer. A really good one. He was part of the US Olympic team in London. Then the trouble started."

"What kind of trouble?"

"He began disappearing. He claimed to hear voices—his devils, he called them. He tried to hurt himself. Doctors diagnosed schizophrenia. They put him on medication and he began to get better. But he had to give up racing. He continued to follow the races and found work as a photographer."

"When I saw him on the surveillance videos, he had a camera."

She closed her eyes, summoning an image of her brother with his camera. In the memory, he was taking pictures of her, laughing and joking around. This was the memory she wanted to keep, not the one of the troubled young man who had left their family so bereft and confused.

She opened her eyes again and found Luke watching her, calm and patient, waiting for more. "We thought everything would be all right," she said. "The medication had side effects—he gained weight, he couldn't sleep—but we thought he had accepted that. That he was building a new life for himself. And then one day he just…vanished."

"No signs of foul play?"

She shook her head. "Later, when we put all the pieces together, I realized there were warning signs—things we ignored because we wanted so desperately for things to be all right. He was unhappy. He stopped socializing with friends. And then we learned he'd stopped seeing his doctors. He didn't refill his medication. He lied to us and told us everything was fine, but we should have known better. We should have seen the signs..."

His hand covered hers, warm and strong, pulling her out of the mire of guilt she'd almost allowed herself to slip back into. "Beating yourself up won't bring him back," he said.

She nodded and gently pulled out of his grasp, though reluctantly. He was so calm and steady, not freaking out at the mention of mental illness and not pulling away from her. She didn't normally associate law enforcement officers with such empathy. The police who had responded when they'd filed a missing persons report on Scott had been coldly suspicious and unhelpful. They didn't have time to waste searching for a twenty-six-year-old who'd decided to drop out of society; especially a twenty-six-year-old who was crazy.

"I'm going to ask you a question that's going to be hard for you to hear," Luke said. "But I want you to answer honestly."

She nodded. Hadn't she already asked a million hard questions of her own over the months since Scott had left?

"Do you think it's possible that your brother has had anything to do with the bombings at bike races?"

"No!"

"But when we spoke yesterday—when I said I was looking for the bomber—that's what you were afraid of, wasn't it? That's why you showed me his picture this morning?"

Reluctantly, she nodded. "I thought you might believe it of him, but I don't believe it," she said. "Scott was never violent toward anyone else. Even when he was at his worst, he only tried to hurt himself, not others."

"Mental illness can make people do things they wouldn't otherwise do," he said. "He may have a grudge against professional cycling since he's no longer able to participate in a sport he loved."

"But you only saw him at the one race, right? He wasn't at the Paris Roubaix, where the first bomb exploded?"

"He wasn't in any of the videos I saw." He didn't add that it was possible her brother had avoided the surveillance cameras; she was grateful for that.

"I don't think he would be comfortable in a place where he didn't speak the language," she said. "Unfamiliar situations upset him, but he knew London from his racing days. He always liked it there."

"Do you think your brother is here, in Denver?" he asked.

She nodded. "He trained in Colorado for the Olympics and he loved it here. For a while, he even talked about moving here. He has friends competing in the race, so that's one more reason for him to be here."

"What will you do if you find him?"

"I think if I could just talk to him, I could

convince him to come home with me. There are other medications he can try, ones without as many side effects. I can help him get better if he'll only give me a chance."

"Do you think he'll listen to you?"

"I hope so. We've always been close. Our mother died when I was seven and Scott was nine. My dad worked a lot, so it was just the two of us a lot of the time. I could always talk to him when no one else could."

"I'll keep an eye out for him, and if I see him, I'll let you know."

"I'd really appreciate it." It was probably the kind of offer anyone would make, but coming from him, it carried more weight. He was going to be looking closely at everyone associated with the race, and since he never forgot a face…

"If you see him, call me at this number." She pulled a pen and notepad from her purse and scribbled her number, then slid the paper across to him.

He studied the number, then folded the paper and tucked it into his pocket. "I guess that's one way to get a pretty woman's phone number," he said.

His teasing tone surprised a laugh from her. She sipped more coffee and pretended to contemplate her now-cold breakfast, though she was really watching him through the screen of her lashes. A man who could make her laugh despite her sadness was remarkable, indeed. "I hope you'll be in touch," she murmured. And not just because of her brother.

Chapter Three

"See anybody familiar?"

"By this time, everyone here is familiar."

"You know what I mean."

"Then, no. I don't see anyone we're looking for." Luke stood with his friend and fellow Search Team member, Special Agent Travis Steadman, outside the hotel ballroom where the banquet to kick off the Colorado Cycling Challenge was set to begin in fifteen minutes. A crush of well-dressed men and women filled the hall, the slender athletes mingling with more robust race fans, national media and a good number of security personnel, both plain-clothes and in uniform.

Scanning the crowd, Luke quickly identified racers, racing fans, hotel personnel and people he'd passed on the street since his arrival in Denver. But the crowd contained none of the suspects the team had identified from surveillance videos. "What about you?" he asked Travis. "Have you seen any of our suspects?"

The tall, laconic Texan frowned. "Not since I spotted Boy Scout in the airport yesterday. I can't believe I let him slip away." The team members had nicknamed the suspect Boy Scout for his slight build and clean-cut good looks.

"He's been either very good or very lucky so far, but he won't get away this time," Luke said. "Not with the team here, actively looking for him."

Travis nodded. "Everything points to him being here. A friend of mine with the Denver

Police said they've heard a lot of rumblings that something big is going to go down at the race."

"Then why not stop the race?" Luke asked. "Why risk lives?"

"The UCI won't do it," Travis said. "When nothing bad happened at the Tour de France this summer, they persuaded themselves they were in the clear. Never mind the intelligence we've received to the contrary."

"Obviously, the feds are overreacting, as usual." Luke repeated the complaint they heard too often in the news.

"The UCI are determined to prove they can run a safe race here in the States," Travis said.

"You can bet it will come back on us if they don't." Luke shoved his hands in his trouser pockets and jingled his change, eyes still sweeping over the crowd. "What if we're wrong and none of our suspects is the bomber?" he asked. "What if it's one of the racers? Or a racing official?"

"The Bureau has other people looking at them," Travis said. "We're focused on the outliers, the people who don't have a logical reason to be at every race where there's been a bomb."

"The people who we were lucky enough to capture on video," Luke said. "I worry about the ones who slip past, unnoticed." He'd let down his guard one time and failed to notice the men who might have the answers to what had happened to his brother. If Luke had been more vigilant, maybe Mark would be home right now with his daughter, instead of "missing, feared dead," as the notation in the police file of his case indicated.

"Our man is here, I know it," Travis said. "Focus on what we can do, not what we can't."

Good advice, though Luke found it hard to implement. He continued to scan the crowd, then stilled as he recognized a familiar blonde head.

"What do you see?" Travis asked. He leaned

closer, following Luke's gaze, then nudged him in the side. "The woman in the blue dress? Definitely a knockout."

Morgan had traded her jeans and tank top for a formfitting evening gown of a shimmery, iridescent blue silk. She carried a cocktail in one hand, a small silver evening bag in the other and turned her head from side to side, as if searching for someone.

"She looks familiar," Travis said. "Someone from our videos?"

"She's a journalist, writes for racing magazines," Luke said. At that moment, Morgan turned in his direction and their eyes met. The now-familiar jolt of connection went through him, and he started toward her.

"Hey, Luke. I was hoping I'd see you here." She touched his arm. "What a crush, huh?"

"Yeah, a lot of people." But he wasn't looking at any of them anymore, only her.

"See anyone, uh, interesting?" Her eyes filled

in the question behind the question—had he seen her brother?

He shook his head, but before he could say more, Travis inserted himself between them. "Since Luke's not going to introduce me, I'll have to do it myself," he said. "I'm Travis Steadman."

"Hello, Mr. Steadman." She shook his hand. "Are you with the FBI, too?"

He grinned. "How did you know?"

"You have that look about you."

"What kind of look?" Luke asked.

"Very official."

"It's an unfortunate side effect of our training," Travis said.

"Are you two headed to Aspen for the first stage of the race tomorrow?" she asked.

Was she making conversation or asking for another reason? Luke hedged his answer. "I'm not sure. What about you? Do you follow the racers around the state?"

She shook her head. "I wish I could, but it's not in my budget. As the racers get closer, I'll make a few day trips, maybe get in a few interviews with the top athletes. But most of the time I can stay in Denver and follow the race on television. At the end of the week, I'll be in a good position to report on the final stage of the race and the results."

Luke liked this answer. Unless his superiors changed their minds, the plan was for him and a few others to stay in Denver all week, as well, while the rest of the team followed the racers. Previously, the bomber had waited until the last day of the races to make his move, when the biggest crowd and the most media coverage were in place. But there was no guarantee he'd stick to that pattern. Meanwhile, maybe Luke and Morgan would have the chance to get to know each other better.

The crowd began to move toward the ballroom doors. "I guess it's time to go in," Travis said.

"May I?" Luke offered Morgan his arm. "That is, if you haven't already arranged to sit with someone else."

"No, um, that would be nice." She laid her hand on his arm, a touch as light as a butterfly, yet he felt it all the way up to his chest. He was definitely in trouble, but he wasn't sure he wanted to get out of it. At least not yet.

By the time they made it inside, most of the tables near the front were already full. Travis steered them toward an empty table at the back, near the kitchen. "Not most people's idea of choice seating," he said, "but it works better for our purposes."

"I get it," she said, as she took the chair Luke held for her. "It's a good place to watch the rest of the crowd."

"She's a fast learner." Travis took the chair

on one side of her, while Luke sat on the other side. "How did you two meet?" Travis asked.

"Um…" She glanced at Luke.

"I recognized her from the surveillance video and started following her," Luke admitted. "She caught me and demanded to know what I was doing."

"She caught you?" Travis grinned. "Didn't we teach you better than that?"

"Ladies and gentlemen, please welcome our mayor." The introduction saved Luke from having to come up with a reply. As they ate their salads, a parade of local dignitaries made speeches praising the athletes, the sponsors, the spectators—pretty much everyone, up to and including the sanitation workers.

"Notice how no one's mentioning the bombings," Travis said.

"I'm sure it's in the back of everyone's mind," Morgan said. "No sense putting more of a damper on the evening by bringing it up."

"Where were you when the bombs went off in London and Paris?" Luke asked.

"You were at those races, too?" Travis was immediately more alert, focused on her. Luke sent him a quelling look.

Morgan didn't appear to notice the exchange. "I was stuck on a shuttle in Paris," she said. "Furious because I was missing the arrival of the winners at the finish line. By the time I got there, the ambulances were carrying away the injured. I realized how lucky I'd been."

"And in London?" Travis asked.

"I was at the finish line, interviewing the leading American racer. We'd moved into the doorway of a building across the street to get out of the sun." Her eyes met Luke's, beautiful and troubled. "The explosion was so loud. It stunned us. We stared at each other and for the longest moment we didn't hear anything else. Then someone screamed, and we knew it had happened again."

He took her hand under the table and squeezed it. "I'm glad you were okay."

"I knew the two racers who died that day," she said. "I had interviewed both of them for an article before the race. They were nice guys, funny and easy to talk to." She shook her head. "I don't understand why anyone would do something like that. Why resort to violence for the sake of violence?"

"Terrorists act to induce fear, and to draw attention to themselves," Travis said.

"But why bicycle races?" she asked.

"It's an international sport," Luke said. "It's popular and draws big crowds. Or maybe this person has a grudge against the sport or the athletes."

"A former racer," she murmured, and he knew she was thinking of her brother.

"It could be anyone." He squeezed her hand. "First we find them, then we worry about their motives."

An army of servers arrived to clear the tables and deliver the entrées—some kind of chicken over rice, in a maroon-colored sauce. Luke leaned over and whispered to Morgan. "Any idea what this is?"

"Not a clue."

Luke ate without tasting the food, one eye on the crowd, the rest of his attention focused on the woman beside him. She was definitely more relaxed now, though with an underlying sadness he understood. Which didn't mean she wasn't involved with the bombings, he reminded himself. But his instincts told him no. She was exactly what she appeared to be: a journalist covering the races, and a sister looking for her missing brother. The two of them had more in common than she knew.

A commotion near the front of the room drew his attention. At the table directly in front of the podium, people were standing. "Someone call an ambulance!" a man shouted.

Luke and Travis rose as one, shoving back their chairs. "What's going on?" Morgan asked, her fork paused, halfway to her mouth.

"We're going to find out," Luke said. He pushed his way toward the front table, Travis on his heels. "Security," he said, flashing his badge when a man tried to block his way.

"What happened?" Travis asked when they reached the table.

"The president has had some kind of attack." The thin-faced man spoke with a French accent.

"I fear he is dead," an older woman in a black evening gown said.

"The ambulance is on its way," the first man said.

Union Cycliste Internationale President Alec Demetrie was a familiar figure to Luke, and to anyone in the professional cycling world. But the inert, ashen-faced man slumped in his chair was almost unrecognizable. Luke felt for a pulse but couldn't find even a flutter. He met Travis's gaze and shook his head.

"What happened?" Luke asked the woman, who he recalled was the president's wife.

She took a deep breath, visibly pulling herself together. "He had a few bites of the entrée and complained of it tasting off. I told him he should send it back to the kitchen, but by then he was already unwell. I tried to get the attention of one of the waiters, then Alec slumped in his chair and…and…" She stared at her husband, unable to say more.

"Paramedics, let us through!"

Luke stepped back to allow two uniformed EMTs to reach the president. He motioned for Travis to follow him some distance away from the table and was surprised when Morgan joined them. "Is he dead?" she asked, keeping her voice low.

Luke nodded. "What do you think?" he asked Travis.

"Maybe he had a heart attack," Travis said. "But I think we'd better make sure someone takes that plate as evidence."

"I overheard what the woman said about the food tasting odd," Morgan said. "Do you think someone poisoned him?"

"I think I'd like to check out the kitchen," Luke said.

"I'll question the waitstaff." Travis nodded toward the dozen or so black-clad servers who stood along the back wall.

Morgan turned to Luke. "I'm coming with you," she said.

"I'd rather you didn't." He didn't like to involve civilians in his work. And if there really was a poisoner in the kitchen, the situation could be dangerous.

"You can't stop me," she said, then slipped her arm in his. "Besides, you're less likely to arouse suspicion in the culprit if you look like a diner interested in complimenting the chef, instead of an FBI agent snooping around."

"I never worry about looking suspicious." But he covered her hand with his own to keep it in place on his arm.

"Right. Because you're an FBI agent and whatever you do is right."

"I didn't say that."

"You didn't have to. I think the attitude comes with the badge."

"You don't look too upset about it."

A sly smile curved her lips. "I like a man with a little attitude."

At the kitchen door, they had to push their way through a crowd of workers who had gathered to view the excitement in the dining room. "What's going on?" asked a man in a white chef's toque and apron.

"One of the diners became ill," Luke said. He scanned the crowd of workers, searching for a familiar face.

Not all the workers had left their duties to gawk at the door. A dishwasher stood with his back to them, rinsing dishes, seemingly oblivious to the commotion. Another worker carried a trash bin to the back door. As he reached the door, the dishwasher moved to open it for him.

Faster than he could articulate the information, Luke's brain processed the data his eyes transmitted: young male, early to midtwenties, slight, athletic build, five-eight or five-nine, clean shaven, short brown hair. "You there, by the door," he called.

The man dropped the trash can and reached behind him. Time slowed as Luke drew his weapon from the holster beneath his jacket. Light glinted off the barrel of the gun the suspect they'd dubbed Boy Scout pulled from his waistband. Morgan screamed, then launched herself toward Luke as shots rang out.

They fell together, Luke propelled backward, crashing against a counter, Morgan sagging against him. Adrenaline flooded his system and he struggled to right himself, gripping his weapon in one hand, pulling Morgan up beside him with the other. "Are you all right?" he demanded, forcing himself to look for the wound he was sure was there.

"I'm sorry." She looked up at him, tears streaking her face. "I had to stop you."

"Are you all right?" he asked again. No blood stained her gown, but he knew the man at the door had been aiming right at them.

"I'm fine." She struggled to pull away from him, but he held her firmly. "I couldn't let you shoot him."

The shooter had missed. Luke glanced toward the back door. Both the men who had been there were gone, the door standing open, the trash can on its side.

He gently set Morgan aside and raced to the door. The alley outside was empty, with no sign of the two men, and no apparent place for them to hide. He pulled out his phone and called his boss. "We've got a shooter on the loose," he said as soon as Blessing answered. "Two men took off on foot from the kitchen of the hotel." He gave a brief description of each man. "I'll be in touch after I've finished assessing the situation here."

He holstered his weapon and returned to the kitchen. Around him, the voices of the others in the room rose, full of questions and protests. He ignored them and found Morgan, standing where he had left her, shoulders hunched, expression stunned. He slipped his arm around her and guided her to a quiet corner. "Who did you think I was shooting at?" he asked.

"The dishwasher. I know you think he's guilty, but he's not. He would never..."

"Shh." He put two fingers to her lips. "I was aiming for the other man. The one by the trash can. Didn't you see the gun in his hand?"

Confusion clouded her eyes. "A gun? I wasn't

looking at him. I was watching the dishwasher. He was…"

"I know." He laid her head against his shoulder and smoothed his hand down her back. "I recognized him, too. He was your brother."

Chapter Four

"What do you think you're doing, you idiot? You can't come in here shooting up my kitchen!" Luke looked up into the florid face of the chef, who held a cleaver in one hand, the other curled into a fist.

"I'm a federal agent." Luke gently separated himself from Morgan. "I have to go," he said, to her, not the cook. "Maybe I can still catch them."

She nodded and pushed him toward the door. "Go. Hurry."

He raced past the gaping chef, skirted the fallen trash can and the lettuce shreds and potato peelings that spilled from it, and pounded into the alley. At the end he looked down the street filled with cars and pedestrians. Taxis and limos jostled for space with more modest sedans across four lanes of traffic idling at the red light on the corner. Half a block farther on, a light rail train blasted its horn as it pulled out of the station. His quarry could be anywhere by now—in one of the taxis or cars, on that train, or hiding in a dark alley nearby.

"You looking for those two who hightailed it out of there a minute ago?"

The raspy tenor voice came from a tall, thin black man who leaned against the brick wall a few feet to Luke's left, one foot propped against the brick, a cigarette glowing in his right hand.

"Which way did they go?" Luke asked.

"Both ways. They split up. Which one did you plan on shooting?"

Luke realized he still held the gun in his right hand. He replaced it in the holster beneath his left arm. "The man with the short brown hair—which way did he go?"

The man straightened, both feet on the ground. "I didn't pay attention to what either of them looked like," he said. "I just know they were bookin' it. I thought I heard gunshots, so I figured I'd best stay out of the way for a while."

"Did you see either of them get into a car or taxi, or onto the train?"

"No. They were both running. I'd just stepped out for a smoke in time to see them leaving." He snuffed out the cigarette against the brick. "And now it's time for me to get back to work." With that, he sauntered back into an alcove and took the stairs down a level to a club, The Purple Martini, spelled out in purple neon above the door.

Luke had little hope of finding either Morgan's brother or his suspect now, but he had to make an effort. He set out walking, past The Purple Martini and a string of closed shops. As he walked, he pulled out his phone and called Travis. "Our suspect got away. He took a shot at me, then ran out the back door. I'm going to show his picture around on the street, but unless we get really lucky, he's gone."

"I heard the shot, but by the time I got to the kitchen it was all over but the crying," Travis said. "The chef is ranting at anyone within earshot and Morgan looks like she's seen a ghost."

"See that she gets back to her hotel okay."

"What happened?" Travis asked.

"I'll tell you the story later. For now, I want to keep looking. It's possible the suspect is still on foot downtown."

"I'm on it."

He ended the call, then scrolled to his photo album. The picture he had of their suspect was a grainy image from a surveillance video, but it showed his face and general build. He approached a group of young people gathered on the corner, waiting for the light to change.

"Have any of you seen this man around to-night?" he asked, holding out his phone.

"Who wants to know?" demanded a beefy blond whose flushed cheeks and bright eyes suggested he'd had a few drinks.

"FBI." Luke flashed his creds and the blond gaped, while his friends crowded close to study first the credentials, then the image on Luke's phone.

One by one they shook their heads. "Sorry."

"No, haven't seen him."

"What's he done?" the blond asked.

"We want to talk to him in connection with a case we're working on."

He moved on to others. Everyone studied the picture, frowning in concentration, but no one remembered seeing the suspect. About the results Luke had expected. Most people didn't really look at others. Even when they did, the details didn't stick in their minds the way they did for Luke.

Over an hour later, he'd covered the two-block area on either side of the hotel with nothing to show for his efforts. He stowed his phone once more and headed back toward the banquet facility. He needed to talk to people there and find out what they knew. Other members of the team had probably already conducted interviews, but he wanted to hear the information firsthand. It was possible the suspect had made friends who knew where he lived. Certainly, they'd have a name, though whether or not it was the man's real identity was doubtful.

And he needed to figure out if Morgan's brother, Scott, had anything to do with the suspect. Maybe he was merely holding the door open for a coworker, but the two had fled together. Luke needed to know why.

A block from the hotel, a woman moved out of the shadows ahead of him. The streetlights shimmered on the blue of her dress, and a gusty breeze tugged at her short hair. Luke straightened. "Morgan, what are you doing here?" he asked.

"I was waiting for you." She moved in close beside him, almost but not quite touching him. She cast a nervous glance over her shoulder toward the front door of the hotel and Luke saw the reason for her nerves: half a dozen news vans crowded the curb and men and women with cameras and microphones filled the portico in front of the entrance, everyone jostling to report the big story of the night.

Luke took her arm and directed her across the street, to a bench at an empty bus stop. "We can talk here," he said. "How are you doing?"

"Okay," she said, though her pinched face and hunched shoulders belied the answer. "Did you find him?"

By "him" did she mean her brother or the suspect? "They both had a big head start on me. I found a witness who said they split up at the end of the alley and ran in opposite directions."

"I'm sure Scott only ran because he was confused and frightened," she said. "He's never liked tense situations, but even more so since he's been diagnosed."

He nodded. "I'd like to talk to him and find out what he knows about my suspect."

"I talked to Gary and he said Scott had been working as a dishwasher only three days," she said.

"Who's Gary?"

"Oh, he's the chef. Gary Forneaux. After you left I offered to bring him a drink from the hotel bar and he calmed down quite a bit. He told me they'd needed extra help for the banquet, so they'd agreed to hire Scott on a trial basis."

"Do you think that's how he's been supporting himself—working temporary jobs in whatever town he's in?"

"Probably. Gary said Scott knew how to run the commercial dishwasher. And he gets along well with most people. He can be very charming when he wants to be. Gary said everyone in the kitchen liked him."

"I'm glad you found him," Luke said. Along with everything else that had happened, there was that one bit of good news for her. "At least you know he's all right."

"But it feels like I've lost him all over again," she said. "No one at the hotel knew where he was staying. Though he did use his real name. Tomorrow I'm going to start calling around to hotels and apartments, trying to find him."

"I hope you do," he said. Not just for his investigation, but because he knew how much being reunited with her lost sibling would mean to her. He would have given almost anything to see Mark again.

"What about the other guy?" he asked. "Did you find out anything about him?"

"His name is Danny. He was a day laborer from a temp agency. He was brought in just for tonight. Gary couldn't even remember his last name and didn't know anything about him."

"Thanks. We'll follow up on it." Though he didn't have high hopes that anyone at the temp agency would have more information. So far this guy had been very good at covering his tracks.

He glanced toward the hotel, at the bright lights and rumbling growl of the generators powering the portable satellite dishes for the news vans. "I guess I'd better get back there."

"Luke." Her hand on his arm drew his attention to her once more. The streetlight overhead cast a golden glow over her, glinting off her hair and shadowing her eyes against her pale skin. "I really don't think Scott knew the man who shot at you. I mean, I don't think they were friends or anything. He was just opening the door for him, not trying to help him escape."

He wrapped his hand around hers and held it to his chest. "I know you want to believe that, but you can't know it. We have to check out the connection, though I hope we don't find one."

"Will you tell me if you do?"

This was hard. He didn't like the thought of keeping anything from her. He knew how much any scrap of information about Mark would mean to him. But he had a job to do. And sometimes that job required making hard decisions. "I can't tell you anything I find," he said. "But I will tell you if we're able to clear your brother."

"So in this case, no news is bad news."

She almost smiled, and the burden of guilt he felt at having to keep things from her lifted a little. He marveled at her ability to maintain a sense of humor under the circumstances. She was stronger than she looked. "You've had a rough night," he said. "You should go back to your hotel and get some sleep."

"What about you?"

"I've still got work to do." He doubted he'd see his bed before morning.

"The first stage of the race starts tomorrow morning, in Aspen," she said. "I have to be up early to Skype into a press conference."

"They're going through with it?"

She nodded. "The UCI made the announcement about an hour ago. The vice president, Pierre Marceau, said it was what Monsieur Demetrie would have wanted."

"So if someone was trying to stop the race by poisoning President Demetrie, he didn't succeed," Luke said.

"Are they sure it was poison?" she asked. "The kitchen was swarming with police after you left. They took leftovers from every dish as evidence. Gary was very upset."

"We'll know by morning, anyway."

"Do you think this is even connected to the bombings?" she asked. "Poisoning seems so personal."

"That's something we'll have to find out." They could very well be looking into two unrelated crimes. He stood, and pulled her up with him. He hated to leave the oasis of this little bench, away from the crowds and all the unanswered questions, but his duty had to come before his personal feelings. "Will you be all right walking to your hotel alone? I can find someone to go with you, but I can't leave the investigation. I've stayed away too long as it is."

"I'll be fine. You've done so much already. Thank you."

"You don't have to thank me." If anything, he'd made things worse for her, placing her brother at the center of an investigation into international terrorism.

"Thank you for listening to me. For believing me—or at least pretending to. And for sharing as much information as you have with me."

"So you aren't afraid of me anymore?" He continued to hold her hand, reluctant to let go.

"No." She put her hand on his chest, the warmth seeping through his shirtfront. "I'm glad we met, in spite of the strange circumstances."

"Yeah. I'm glad, too." Maybe from the moment he'd first seen her in that video, he'd known he'd seek her out. Something in her called to him.

She tilted her head up and rose on her toes to bring her face closer to his in silent invitation—an invitation he wouldn't refuse. He'd been wanting to kiss her, hesitant only because of the tenuousness of their relationship. Her lips warmed beneath his, as soft and sensuous as he'd imagined they would be. He wrapped his arms around her to pull her closer and she slid one hand around to cup the back of his head, her fingers tangled in his hair. He stroked his tongue along the seam of her mouth and she opened for him with a soft sigh more passionate than any words would have been. Every nerve in his body was attuned to her, to the soft floral aroma of her perfume, to the taste of wine that lingered on her lips, to the curve of her breasts against his chest and the strong line of her spine beneath his hand. He deepened the kiss, lost in the sensation of her.

A flash of light to his left distracted him, and reluctantly he lifted his head to look around, a sleeper emerging from a wonderful, compelling dream. He saw nothing but the array of news vans and reporters across the street, though he couldn't shake the sense that something had happened that he should have paid attention to.

"I'd better go. Good night."

She slipped from his arms and he curled his fingers into his palms to keep from pulling her back. She gave him a shy smile, then turned and walked away, hips swaying in the blue silk as she walked briskly down the sidewalk. He watched until she'd disappeared in a crowd at the corner, then turned toward the hotel to face a long night of unanswered questions.

THE MEMBERS OF Search Team Seven assembled the next morning in a conference room in the hotel that had hosted the banquet the night before. Luke slid into the seat next to Travis and nodded a silent greeting to the other team members. They all looked as weary and frustrated as he felt. Across from Luke, Gus Mathers stared at his phone, his eyes half-closed behind his black-framed hipster glasses. Next to him, Jack Prescott's burly frame looked too big for the spindly folding chair. Farther down the table, the youngest members of the team, Wade Harris and Cameron Hsung, cupped hands around the takeout coffee they'd brought in. Even in their regulation suits, they managed to look like the college students they had been until only a few months before.

The door opened and Ted Blessing strode in. He'd flown in on a red-eye and wore the look of a man who wasn't happy about having his sleep disturbed. In his midforties, with mud-brown skin and closely cropped hair that showed no sign of gray, he favored tailored suits and had the ramrod-straight spine of the military officer he'd been before joining the Bureau. He laid a tablet computer on the conference table in front of him and studied his team, all of whom were now sitting up straight and at attention.

"How is it that this man keeps getting away, when there are six of you and only one of him?" Blessing asked.

The others cast furtive glances at one another. It wasn't a question that had a good answer—or any answer. As usual, Jack was the first to speak. "He's got to have accomplices, helping him get away," he said. "Someone with a car waiting for him, and a safe place for him to hole up."

"We're circulating his picture to all local law enforcement," Wade said. "They'll be on the lookout for him."

"He'll dye his hair or put on glasses and they won't recognize him if they trip over him," Cameron said. Such disguises rarely fooled the recognizers on the team—they memorized facial composition, mannerisms and other details that couldn't be hidden so easily.

"I don't want some local cop to nail him," Gus said. "I want to nail him."

The others murmured agreement. Blessing sat, hands clasped on the table in front of him. "Let's go over what we know so far. Agent Steadman?"

Travis referred to the tablet in front of him. "We know our suspect was going by the name Danny in the hotel kitchen, but we're pretty confident that isn't his real name. We spoke with the day labor organization that supplies temp workers to the hotel. The supervisor tells me that a Danny Robinson, a sometimes homeless man with a history of alcoholism, was the man who was supposed to report for work in the hotel kitchen that night."

"His body was found wrapped in a tarp and stuffed in a culvert near Confluence Park, not far from downtown Denver." Cameron picked up the story. "His throat was cut. We believe our suspect murdered him and took the hotel job in his stead, in order to get close to UCI officials."

"The chicken that President Demetrie ate tested positive for potassium cyanide," Jack said. "We should have the autopsy results later this morning, but it looks like that's what did him in. There was enough potassium cyanide in the dish that only a few bites would result in death within minutes."

"Did cyanide show up on any of the other plates?" Blessing asked.

Jack shook his head.

"So President Demetrie was definitely the target," Gus said.

"We don't think so," Travis said. "The covered plates with the entrées were stacked on trays and sent out by table. So the poisoner had a reasonably good chance of knowing that this plate would go to one of the tables of dignitaries seated at the front of the room, nearest the dais. But without the cooperation of the server, there was no way to be certain who would get that particular plate."

"So maybe the server helped him out," Blessing said.

"I spoke to the man who served that table," Travis said. "He's a longtime employee at the hotel. He says he never met our suspect, and witnesses back up his story. We're still investigating, but if our suspect had help, I don't think it was the server."

"What about the other guy in the kitchen— the dishwasher?" Cameron asked. "He and the suspect left together, right?"

Luke shifted and all eyes turned to him. "The dishwasher's name is Scott Westfield," he said. "He's a former pro cyclist who had to retire due to a medical condition. Since then, he's traveled around, taking a series of odd jobs. He sometimes photographs races."

"What kind of medical condition?" Blessing asked.

"He was diagnosed with schizophrenia."

"So, we've got a former racer, possibly upset at being made to retire, who's mentally unstable." Jack ticked the facts off on his fingers. "Sounds like the kind of guy who'd be happy to help our suspect. Maybe he's even the one behind the bombings and our suspect is secondary."

"I don't think so." Luke hadn't meant to speak up in Scott's defense. After all, the evidence pointing to his involvement in the bombings was pretty damning. But Morgan's faith in her brother had swayed him. "I can't find any connection between Westfield and our suspect. Westfield had been working in the hotel kitchen a couple of days before our suspect hired on, and the rest of the staff didn't notice any particular friendship between them."

"That kind of thing is easy enough to hide," Wade said. "Westfield gets the job first to scope the place out, then our suspect joins him. The fact that they left together tells me they were working as a team."

"Maybe," Luke conceded. "We need to find Westfield and question him."

"Oh, we'll have plenty of questions for him," Blessing said. He leaned forward. "But let's not lose sight of the bigger picture here. We've got some intel pointing to a possible terrorist cell, possibly based here in Colorado."

"What kind of intel?" Luke asked, relieved that the focus had shifted away from Morgan's brother, at least for the moment.

"Some intercepted phone conversations that seem to point to a plan to sabotage transportation hubs in the region, and a report of suspicious activity at a private airport near Denver that was called in by a concerned citizen." Blessing's expression grew more grim. "Nothing concrete, but it's worth paying attention to. We've got people working to follow these leads. For now, your job is to focus on finding our suspect and Scott Westfield. Don't let them get away this time." He stood, signaling the meeting was at an end, and the others rose, also. "Someone bring me the local papers. I want to see what the press is saying about all this."

As Luke turned toward the door, Blessing stopped him. "Agent Renfro, stay and talk to me for a minute."

Travis gave him a sympathetic look as he filed out with the others, leaving Luke alone with his commander. "Sit down." Blessing indicated the chair to his right.

Luke sat. He could guess what this was about. Discharging his weapon in public was serious enough to warrant a private briefing if not disciplinary action. Filing a report about the incident was at the top of his to-do list today.

Blessing fixed him with a steady, calm gaze. "I know what others say happened in the kitchen last night, but I want to hear it from you. I expect your written report later, but tell me now, in your own words."

Luke shifted, as if there was any way to get comfortable on the receiving end of a grilling from his boss. "After the president's death, I went to the kitchen to question the staff," he said.

"You weren't alone."

"No, sir."

"Witnesses say you were with a woman. Who was that?"

"Her name is Morgan. Morgan Westfield. She's a magazine writer."

He could sense Blessing grow more alert, like a hound on the scent of a quarry. "Any relation to the dishwasher?"

"He's her brother. Though I didn't know that when I went into the kitchen."

"How do you know Ms. Westfield?"

"We met in the lobby of her hotel the day before yesterday. I recognized her from some of the surveillance videos from the races and decided to follow her."

"Do you think she's involved in the bombings somehow? Perhaps she and her brother are part of this cell we're looking for."

Luke shook his head. "I followed her because I wasn't sure of anything at that point. I just wanted to check her out." Not the entire truth but close enough. "But now I'm convinced she was at the races for her job and nothing else."

"And you know this how?"

"Everything she told me checked out. She's at the races on assignment for *Road Bike Magazine*, and she's blogging for a website, Cycling-Pro.com." Though he hadn't contacted anyone at the magazine to verify that. Was he letting his attraction to Morgan—his desire for her to be innocent—get in the way of doing his job?

"What was she doing with you last night?"

"We sat together at dinner. She followed me into the kitchen."

Blessing's face betrayed no emotion, but Luke could sense his skepticism. "Go on."

"I recognized the man who was carrying out the garbage as one of our suspects. I spoke to him and he pulled a gun. I pulled my weapon and returned his fire. He fled out the door."

"Is that all?"

"No, sir." The truth was bound to come out

sooner or later, if it hadn't already. Half a dozen people had been working in the kitchen last night and team members had interviewed all of them. "As I pulled my weapon, Ms. Westfield shoved me out of the way. We both fell to the floor, which gave the suspect time to flee."

"Why did she push you?"

"She didn't understand why I was shooting. She saw my gun and panicked."

"Or she knew exactly what you were doing and acted to stop you."

"Yes, sir. That is a possibility." One he couldn't idly set aside. He was trained to be skeptical and suspicious. He couldn't set that training aside because of his attraction to Morgan.

"You realize what you've done, Renfro?" Blessing's voice held a sharp edge; Luke felt the cut. He said nothing but forced himself to look his boss in the eye.

"At worst, you've become involved with the

very person you're supposed to bring to justice. At best, you've endangered a civilian and jeopardized this investigation."

"Yes, sir." Luke held himself rigid.

"I expect better of you. You're not some randy teenager controlled by your hormones. If this woman is guilty, she's playing you for a fool and possibly using you to help her commit acts of terrorism. If she's innocent, she's interfering with a critical investigation. You're here to work, Renfro, not enjoy yourself."

"Yes, sir."

A knock on the conference room door preempted anything else Blessing was about to say. "Come in," he barked.

Wade entered the room. As he passed, he gave Luke a sympathetic look. "You asked to see the local papers," he said to Blessing.

"Sir, may I get back to work now?" Luke asked, seeing his chance for escape.

"Yes, go," Blessing said. He unfolded the first

newspaper on the stack. "But remember your focus here. Don't let yourself get distracted again."

"Yes, sir." Luke started toward the door. He had his hand on the knob when Blessing barked his name again.

"Renfro!"

Luke turned, heart pounding. "Yes, sir?"

"How do you explain this?" Blessing turned the paper to face Luke, who stared at the picture at the bottom of the page, of him and Morgan standing in the bus shelter, wrapped in a passionate kiss. Love Amidst the Chaos, read the caption.

Chapter Five

Morgan logged out of Skype after the UCI press conference. Interim President Pierre Marceau had delivered an impassioned address about the importance of continuing to uphold the honorable tradition of their sport in the wake of tragedy. He would not disrespect the athletes who had worked so hard to get here or disappoint the fans who had rallied around them. The death of President Demetrie might not even be connected to the previous bombings. It would be a mistake to overreact to what might only be an unfortunate accident. But even if the president's tragic demise was the work of those who had set out to destroy racing, the UCI would not give in to the threats of terrorists. The cycling community was stronger than the faceless cowards who had targeted past races. With heightened security and eternal vigilance they would all emerge victorious from this race.

The crowds gathered in Aspen for the start of the race had cheered wildly at the end of the speech, and the racers had set off on the first of what would be seven stages covering almost eleven hundred kilometers through some of Colorado's most scenic and challenging terrain. They would arrive back in Denver on Sunday for the final stage to determine the winner. Morgan had agreed to write a short article for a bicycling website about the death of UCI President Demetrie, and another piece about this morning's press conference, but she wasn't anxious to get started on that work. She couldn't sit still in front of a computer, knowing that Scott was so close—almost within her reach.

And she needed to find him before Luke or one of his fellow FBI agents arrested him for something he hadn't done. No way was Scott a terrorist. No matter what schizophrenia had done to his brain, she refused to believe her brother would ever harm anyone else.

At the hotel where the banquet had been held, she bypassed the front entrance and made her way to the alley and the door into the kitchen. The scents of cooking onion, garlic and peppers engulfed her as she stepped inside, making her mouth water. The chaos of the previous evening had been replaced by a different kind of busyness. Sometime in the night, workers had cleared away all evidence of the police presence and restored order to the kitchen. The chef, Gary, presided over an army of men and women who chopped, sautéed, plated and cleared dishes for late-breakfast or early-lunch diners and room service orders.

But Scott was nowhere among the crowds of workers. A young woman with spiked hair had assumed his place in front of the commercial dishwasher. Trying to hide her disappointment, Morgan made her way into the kitchen. When Gary saw her, a grin split his face. "Hey, girl," he said. "What brings you back here this morning? You looking for a job?"

She managed a smile and shook her head. "I was hoping to see Scott," she said.

"He hasn't come in yet, and we could really use the help. We got behind, what with dealing with the cops and all." His sunny expression clouded. "I can't believe those clowns. They practically accused me of poisoning that man. As if I would do something like that."

"So he *was* poisoned?" She moved to join him in front of the massive commercial range, where he sautéed mounds of chopped vegetables in a large skillet.

"Cyanide." Gary's eyes widened. "Can you believe? Nasty stuff."

"That is bad." And it explained why Monsieur Demetrie had perished so quickly. "Say, Gary, do you know how I can get in touch with Scott? Where he lives or a phone number or anything?"

"Sorry, sweetie, I don't." He added the contents of a measuring cup to the skillet and clouds of fragrant steam momentarily obscured his face. "I don't ask too many questions about the people who work for me," he said. "It's usually better that way."

That was probably why Scott had been drawn to kitchen work, she thought. He'd always been a very private person, and more so since his diagnosis.

"You have good timing," Gary said, looking over her shoulder. "Look who just walked in."

She turned in time to see Scott tying on a big white apron. He didn't glance in her direction—or at anyone else, for that matter, but moved to the sink and began rinsing the pile of dishes there.

She hurried to his side. "Hi, Scott," she said softly, afraid of frightening him away.

He cut his eyes in her direction and quickly looked away.

"It's good to see you," she said. He looked the same as he always had—thin and wiry, a bicyclist's body even two years after he'd stopped competing. "How have you been?"

"Okay." She waited for him to ask about her or their father and stepmother, but he didn't.

"I've missed you," she said. "Dad and Nicole miss you, too. I'd love it if you'd come home with me for a visit."

He jerked his head back and forth, almost violently. "No. Won't go back."

"You don't have to do anything you don't

want to do," she said. "But why wouldn't you want to come home, just for a visit? To let Dad and Nicole know you're okay."

"I'm not supposed to go home. The demons tell me not to."

"Aw, honey." She stroked his arm. "We can find some new medication that will shut those demons up for good. Drugs without all the side effects you had problems with before."

He set his mouth in a stubborn line and said nothing, focusing on the dishes.

She tried another tack. "What brought you to Denver?" she asked.

"I came for the race."

"That's good. Have you seen some friends while you're here?"

"Some." His expression grew more troubled. "They're all busy. Still racing. I think it was a bad idea for me to come. I should leave."

"Please don't go before we've had a chance to catch up." She tried not to sound as desperate as she felt. If she talked to him longer, reminded him of how close they had been, maybe she could convince him to ignore the voices in his head and listen to her instead.

He switched off the water and turned to her, looking her in the eye for the first time. "What were you doing with that guy last night?" he asked. "The guy with the gun."

"I was looking for you."

"Why? Do you think I did something wrong? I didn't." He flinched, clearly agitated, and began shaking his head again.

"I know that. You wouldn't do anything wrong. I just wanted to see you. Because you're my brother and I love you."

"That guy had a gun," he said.

She debated whether to tell Scott that Luke was a law enforcement officer. Would that frighten him even more? "He was looking for the man who was taking out the trash," she said. "Are you a friend of his?" Her stomach knotted as she waited for his answer.

"Danny?" He shook his head, then nodded. "I mean, I didn't really know him. I ran into him in London. He was watching the race. A fan, you know?"

"So he likes racing, too. That's something you have in common."

"But we're not friends or anything. He scares me."

He switched on the water again and reached for a dirty plate.

"Why does he scare you?" she asked. "Did he threaten you or try to hurt you?"

"He put something on one of the plates last night. He didn't think anyone saw him, but I did. And when he looked around and saw me watching, he made a really mean face. It scared me."

"Hey, sweetie, I'm sorry to break this up, but you're gonna have to go." Gary joined them by the sink. "We're getting ready for the lunch rush and I need Scott to speed it up on washing these dishes."

She started to protest but thought better of it. She didn't want to get on Gary's bad side. "Okay, I'll go now." She pulled a business card from her pocket and scribbled the name of her hotel, her room number and her cell number on the back. "Come see me after you get off, okay?" she said, slipping the card into the back pocket of Scott's jeans. "We'll have dinner and just talk. Okay?"

He nodded, head down over the sink.

She wished he would look at her so she could see that he really meant to stop by later. But he clearly didn't intend to look up, and she could feel Gary growing impatient. She patted Scott's shoulder. "See you later."

She stopped at the door and glanced back at him. He'd looked up from the sink and was watching her. The haunted look in his eyes made her want to cry out and rush to his side to comfort him. But she knew doing so would only make him retreat further into his shell. So she settled for a brave smile and a wave, then hurried away, blinking back the tears that stung her eyes.

LUKE'S FACE STILL burned from the tongue-lashing he'd endured from Blessing when he finally exited the conference room. Fury churned his stomach and knotted his fists. He didn't know whether he was more upset with Blessing, the photographer who'd snagged the damning photo, Morgan for interfering with his case or himself, for getting involved in such a mess.

Travis caught up with him at the elevators. "What happened in there?" he asked.

Luke shoved both hands in his pockets. "I'm off the case."

Travis had the grace to look stunned. "Why?"

"Did you see the paper?"

"The picture of you and Morgan? Yeah. Some photographer's idea of being cute."

"Blessing is hot under the collar about it. Says I jeopardized the case, endangered a civilian. He's pulling me off."

"Off the team?"

"No." At least the commander hadn't gone that far. "He's shifting me to tracking down leads on the terrorist cell, trying to find a connection."

"Maybe you'll have better luck than we've had. Our guy has vanished, and Blessing isn't the only one losing patience."

"All the more reason why I should be out pursuing our suspect. I was the closest to him. I got the best look."

"You'll still be in the loop, so you can help us," Travis said. "Will you see Morgan again?"

"I still have a lot of unanswered questions for her." The elevator arrived and he stepped on. Alone after the doors closed, those questions played on an endless loop in his head. Was Morgan spinning a crazy lie for him? Were she and her brother somehow tied up in terrorist activity? Was she using him to keep tabs on the investigation?

The pain when she'd talked about her missing brother had felt so real to him. It was the same pain he felt when he thought of Mark. But was he letting his emotions interfere with logic? The other team members didn't have any trouble thinking of Morgan as a suspect—why couldn't he reclaim that same objectivity?

As if his thoughts had summoned her, when he stepped off the elevator, Morgan was standing there, waiting to get on. She grabbed his arm, practically vibrating with excitement. "I saw Scott," she said. "I talked to him. He agreed to have dinner with me after he gets off tonight."

Out of the corner of his eye he spotted Cameron, in line at the lobby coffee shop. He hadn't seen Luke yet, but all he had to do was turn his head to spot him talking with a woman the rest of them hadn't ruled out as a suspect. Luke hurried her out of sight, around the corner. "We need to go somewhere we can talk," he said. "Somewhere private."

"Have you found out something? Something about Scott? Or about Danny?"

"I'll tell you what I can when we're alone." He scanned the area. Any minute now, Blessing himself might walk around the corner and see them.

"All right," she said. "Do you want to come to my hotel? We'll have plenty of privacy in my room."

He knew she didn't mean anything illicit in the invitation, so why did his mind go immediately to images of them sharing a bed? As if that was the only reason two adults might be alone in a hotel room in the middle of the day. "All right," he said. "Lead the way."

LUKE SAID NOTHING on the walk over to Morgan's hotel, and as they rode the elevator up to her floor, he kept his eyes focused on the door in front of them. His silence and his refusal to look at her made the distance between them seem much greater than the few inches that physically separated them.

She led the way down the hall to her room, aware of his muffled tread on the carpeting behind her. "This is it," she said, stopping in front of the door, nerves making her hand shake as she slid her key card into the lock. She'd felt so at ease with Luke last night, but something had happened to change that. Not knowing what that something was made her uneasy.

Inside, she was relieved to see that the maid service had made the bed and provided fresh towels. Being here alone with Luke was awkward enough without an unmade bed to taunt them. And why did hotel rooms never have adequate seating? With only one chair, one of them was going to have to sit on the bed.

It didn't help when Luke took the Do Not Disturb sign and hung it on the doorknob. "I don't want any interruptions," he said.

A hot tremor raced up her spine at the words, as if her body insisted on seeing this meeting as a passionate tryst even though her mind knew differently. She backed toward the bed but didn't sit. "Is something wrong?" she asked.

"Why would you think something was wrong?" His words were clipped, his tone bitter.

"You're acting strange," she said. "As if you're angry at me."

"I'm angry at you. And at myself. And at pretty much everyone else involved in this whole fiasco of a case." He raked one hand through his hair and looked around the room, as if searching for something to punch.

"What's wrong?" She did sit then, her legs too shaky to support her. "What's happened?"

"I've been pulled off the case. I'm lucky I wasn't sent back to Washington, or to Timbuktu."

She had trouble breathing, and it was a moment before she could speak. "Pulled off the case? Why?"

The grieved look in his eyes wounded her. "You don't know? You can't guess?"

"Was it because I interfered with your capturing the terrorist?" The memory of that made her stomach hurt. "I feel terrible about that, but I didn't know—"

"Have you seen today's paper?"

She shook her head, confused.

He strode to the laptop set up on her desk and stabbed at the keys. After a moment, he angled the screen toward her.

She stared at the image that filled the screen, of them clinging together, bodies melded, lips joined. Her body responded with the same heat and intense desire she had felt in his arms, sensuous and visceral. Then the realization of what he was showing snapped her back to the present. "Someone took our picture? Why?"

"I thought maybe you knew."

"No, I… That was in the paper?"

"Front page. Love Amidst the Chaos." His scowl chilled her.

"I had no idea…"

"You swear you didn't know anything about this?" He jabbed his finger at the screen.

"Of course not. What? Do you think I arranged for someone to take our picture? Why would I do that?"

"You must have photographer friends. If you thought I was getting too close to information you didn't want me to have, you might use this kind of publicity to get me pulled from the case."

"Excuse me, but I don't recall holding a gun

to your head and forcing you to kiss me. And what do you mean, 'information I didn't want you to have'? What are you talking about?"

"I'm talking about the way your involvement in this case looks when I lay out the facts."

She folded her arms across her chest. It was either that or give in to the urge to slap him. But she wasn't the slapping kind. "What facts are those?"

"When I went into the hotel kitchen last night to ask questions, you insisted on coming with me. Your brother, who you claim not to have seen for months, just happens to be there." He paced the narrow space between the bed and desk, ticking off his reasons on his fingers. "You say you didn't even notice the other man who was there, the one who tried to shoot me, but your pushing me out of the way allowed him to get away—and your brother with him. When I returned from searching for them last night, you just happened to be waiting to find out what I knew. And that kiss we shared got me pulled from the case, so I'm no longer part of the search for your brother or our other suspect."

"You're forgetting one very important *fact*. You're the one who approached me first. I came here to write a story for a magazine and the next thing I know, an FBI agent is following me. How, exactly, do you think I arranged for that to happen?"

Some of the stiffness went out of his posture. "Maybe you only saw your chance after I approached you."

"Right. Because, obviously, I'm a criminal genius. Then how about this? My brother really has been missing for ten months. You can check the missing person's report in Austin. Or talk to my parents, who are beside themselves because they haven't known where their son is. Or you could talk to Scott's doctors."

"You and your brother could have planned

this all ahead of time." But even he didn't sound that convinced of the words.

"Fine. You believe all the lies you want to. But I'm not the one with the problem here—you are." She jabbed her finger at his chest. "Your trouble is you don't trust anyone."

"I've learned not to trust people. My line of work teaches us that trust is dangerous."

"Everything I did—all those *facts* you think are so incriminating—I did to protect my brother. If you had a brother, you'd understand."

"I do have a brother. And I understand more than you know." The weight of emotion behind his words froze her. She studied his face: aged by grief, the sadness in his eyes the same she saw in the faces of her parents and in her own reflection when she looked in the mirror during unguarded moments.

She carefully lowered herself to the bed once more, her outrage receding in the face of his sorrow, and patted the place beside her. "Tell me about your brother," she said.

He sat and leaned forward, elbows on his knees, head bowed. "His name is Mark. We're twins—fraternal, not identical. He's a physicist at the University of Colorado in Boulder. Or he was before he disappeared."

"Oh." The cry escaped her before she could repress it. "How long has he been missing?"

"Almost a year now. He went on a solo hike in the mountains and never came back. When search parties didn't find him, local authorities assumed he'd fallen or gotten lost and perished. Others suggested he committed suicide. His wife had been killed in a car accident six months before and he was still grieving for her."

"But you don't believe that." She touched his arm, wanting to comfort him. More than one cop had suggested her brother had gone away somewhere to kill himself.

Luke straightened. "No, I don't. For one thing, he has a little girl he adored. Mindy is five. After his wife Christy's death, she became even more important to Mark. He would never have deliberately left her an orphan."

"Where is she now?"

"She lives with her godmother, Christy's sister. She doesn't believe her father is dead, either. She told Susan, her aunt, that she has dreams about him, and that she knows he's going to come back to her."

Her hand tightened around his arm and she tried to force down the lump in her throat.

"There's another reason I believe he's still alive," Luke said. "After he disappeared, I found out he'd been receiving threats."

"What kind of threats?"

"Vague ones. Some of them threatened him, some targeted Christy. They said harm would come to her if he didn't cooperate." He shook his head. "I don't know why he didn't tell me about them. Maybe he thought knowing would put me in danger, but I could have investigated. I had all the resources of the Bureau at my disposal."

"Were you able to find out anything more after he was gone?" she asked.

"No. Although some of the messages seemed to suggest that Christy's death might not have been the accident it seemed. I tried to look into that, but I didn't get very far."

"Do you think he was kidnapped?" *Or murdered?* She didn't say those last words out loud. She wouldn't add to his burden.

"I think so. The worst thing is, I might have been in a position to stop it—or at least to find the people who did it." He turned to her, anguish written on his face. "I dropped him off at the trailhead the morning he set out on his hike. There was another car already there, with two men also getting ready to hit the trail. If I'd paid more attention—if I'd taken even a few more seconds to memorize their faces—I might be able to find them now."

"Don't do that," she said, her voice sharper than she'd intended.

"Do what?"

"Don't beat yourself up that way. I've done it and it doesn't do anything but make you feel worse. It doesn't help your brother. How many times do you think I've replayed my last visit with Scott over and over in my head? Why didn't I see how unhappy he was? Why didn't I offer to help him? Why didn't I find him the answers he needed? But none of us are mind readers. We can't see the future. Neither one of us had any way of knowing what would happen."

"You're right." He covered her hand with his. "Thanks for understanding. And I'm sorry I went off on you earlier. I shouldn't have taken my frustrations with the case out on you."

She gently slipped her hand from beneath his.

For a moment she'd forgotten the rift between them and felt the closeness that had drawn her to him in the first place. "I guess I'd rather know you have doubts about me than be unsure of your feelings."

"No." He captured her hand in his once more. "Laying everything out like that helped me see the holes in any theory I might have had about you being part of this. I would have come to the same conclusion, eventually, if I'd been thinking clearly."

"But your colleagues still think I'm suspect."

"Right now, we're all in the mode of checking out any lead, no matter how tenuous, in hopes of finding a way to our suspect. We don't want more lives lost in another act of terrorism." He released her again. "I really need to talk to your brother, to find out anything at all he might know about this Danny character. Do you think you could persuade him to talk to me?"

"Maybe." She shifted, torn between protecting Scott and helping Luke. But somehow, in the past forty-eight hours, her feelings had grown to the point where she didn't think she could keep anything important from him. "He told me he knew Danny from before. Not well, but he said he'd run into him in London."

"Was he calling himself Danny there, too? Did Scott say what he was doing there?"

"He said Danny was a race fan, but I don't know how much interaction they had. Scott was at work, so we couldn't talk long. But he promised to come to my room after he got off work tonight so we could talk."

"I could question him."

"No. You'll scare him off. He's really suspicious of strangers."

"You could tell him I was a friend of yours."

She smiled. "He picked up on the fact that we were together. I couldn't tell if he liked that or not. He's always been protective of me. But I'll try to persuade him to at least meet you.

There's something else he told me—something that might be even more important to your case."

"What's that?"

"He said he saw Danny put something in the food on one of the plates last night, right before it went out to the servers."

"What did he put in there?"

"Scott didn't say. He said Danny saw him watching, though, and threatened him. Scott was really frightened, so that's something else that points to them not working together."

"Then it's even more important that I talk to Scott. We need to persuade him to let us bring him into protective custody."

"Custody? Why? He hasn't done anything wrong."

"No. But if the suspect knows that Scott could testify against him in this poisoning case, your brother could be in real danger."

She put her hand to her chest, pressing down

on the stab of pain there, then realized she had stopped breathing. She struggled to take a breath, her heart hammering. "You think Danny might harm him?"

"If the man doesn't have any qualms about hurting dozens of innocent people with a bomb or poisoning a race official, he wouldn't blink at getting rid of a dishwasher he thought might cause him trouble." He put his arm around her and pulled her close. "I don't mean to frighten you. We'll do everything we can to protect your brother, but he has to cooperate with us."

She nodded, grateful for the strength of his arm around her. "I'll talk to him. I'll try to make him see how important it is to trust us."

His phone vibrated, making her jump. He slipped the device from his pocket and glanced at the screen. "I have to take this," he said, and stood.

She rose, also, and went to the laptop, closing the window with the picture of her and Luke kissing, but not before studying it a moment longer. That had been such an intense, private moment. She felt a little violated, having their shared passion exposed to the world. All because some photographer thought it would make a nice—or maybe titillating?—contrast to the other scenes of violence on the page.

Luke grabbed her arm, startling her. "We've got to get over to the hotel kitchen right away," he said.

"What? Why?" She tried to resist as he tugged her toward the door.

"That call was from Travis. He just got word that one of the dishwashers is brandishing a knife, threatening to use it if anyone comes near him."

Chapter Six

Travis met Luke and Morgan outside the kitchen after they'd rushed down the street and worked their way through a gauntlet of press, hotel employees and local cops. "What's going on?" Luke asked.

"One of the kitchen help, a dishwasher, lost it. He's holed up in an alcove by the sinks, brandishing a knife and threatening to cut anyone who comes near him."

Morgan clutched Luke's hand and let out a soft moan. He stayed focused on Travis but squeezed her hand to let her know he was aware of her distress. "Do you have a name on this guy?" he asked.

"Scott. Is that the guy who ran with the suspect last night?"

"He ran the same time as the suspect, not with him," Luke said.

"Scott is my brother," Morgan said. She was pale, but her voice was steady and she'd let go of Luke's hand. "I can get him to calm down, I'm sure."

"Has he ever done anything like this before?" Luke asked.

She worried her bottom lip between her teeth, then gave one quick jerk of her head. "Once. Before he was diagnosed. Not with a knife, but a couple of years ago, he barricaded himself behind a table in a pizza place where he used to hang out. He had a pool cue and told everyone they had to stay away."

"What happened then?" Travis asked.

"I convinced him to come out. The local

cops—guys he knew—took him to a hospital. That's where he was diagnosed."

Travis glanced toward the closed kitchen door. "There are a couple of local officers in there with him now. I told them we had someone coming who might be able to help, so I think they'll let you talk to him, but it's their call."

Luke put a hand at her back. "I'll go in with you. If you can convince him to put the knife down and cooperate, he'll have to go to the hospital again." He didn't mention the possibility of custody and criminal charges; in any case, that wasn't his decision to make.

"The best thing for him would be to get help and medication," she said.

Luke nodded to Travis. "I think we're ready."

Inside the kitchen, they were met by a young woman in a black pantsuit and an older man with the build of a former football player. They introduced themselves as Lieutenant Litchfield and Detective Young of the Denver PD. "Detective Young is one of our hostage negotiators," Litchfield said.

"Does he have a hostage?" Morgan's voice carried a note of panic.

"Thankfully, no." Detective Young's hazel eyes assessed Morgan. "I'm here to try to talk him into putting down the knife and coming with us quietly," she said.

"This is Morgan Westfield," Luke said. "She's the young man's sister. She believes he'll listen to her and cooperate."

"Any idea what brought this on?" Litchfield asked. "Does he have a history of this kind of behavior?"

"He was diagnosed two years ago with schizophrenia." Morgan kept her gaze focused at the back of the kitchen, though the sink area wasn't visible from where they were standing. "He hears voices and gets upset about things sometimes. Please, let me talk to him."

"All right," Detective Young said. "But don't get too close until he agrees to put down the knife. We don't want this to turn into a hostage situation." She led them toward the back of the room. They turned a corner and the alcove came into view.

Scott crouched on the floor in front of the big sink, one arm hugging his knees. In his free hand, he clutched a chef's knife. His head jerked up at their approach, and he waved the knife, though he remained on the floor. "Don't come any closer!" His voice was high-pitched and agitated.

"It's me, Scott. Morgan." She bent over, leaning toward him. "I just want to talk to you."

"Go away!" he shouted.

"I will, if you really want me to. But, first, tell me what's wrong." Morgan's voice was gentle, full of sympathy.

"I just want people to leave me alone," Scott

said. His face was angled toward her, his gaze unfocused, his eyes darting and fearful.

"Who is bothering you?" Morgan asked.

"Everyone. They keep looking at me and saying things."

"Is it the devils, Scott? Are they bothering you?"

He pressed his lips together and shook his head, then nodded.

"I think we can make them stop," Morgan said. She took a step toward her brother. Luke tried to pull her back, but she shook him off. "If you'll put down the knife and come with me, I promise to help."

"No. Don't come any closer."

She froze as he waved the knife. Luke kept his hands at his sides, poised to retrieve her if necessary. "You know I would never hurt you," Morgan said. "And I'd never let anyone else hurt you."

"Who's that?" Suddenly alert, Scott glared at Luke and jabbed the knife in his direction.

"That's my friend Luke. He wants to help you, too."

"He has a gun."

Detective Young gave Luke a questioning look, but he ignored her.

"Luke only uses his gun to hunt bad guys," Morgan said. "He knows you're not a bad guy."

He wished he did know that. For her sake, at least.

"Bad guy. Bad guy. Bad guy," Scott droned.

Morgan glanced back at them, beautiful even in her anguish. "Maybe I'd better take over," Detective Young said. She started to step forward, but Morgan waved her away.

"Just give me a minute more," she said. She looked back at Scott. "I was thinking about you the other day," she said.

Scott said nothing and gave no indication he'd even heard her. She took a step closer. "I was remembering when we were kids. Do you remember the neighbor we had—the old man who was so mean to all us kids?"

"Mr. Invin."

"That's right. We all waited for the school bus on the corner by his house and he was always accusing us of throwing trash in his yard and riding our bikes across his grass."

"And picking his pears," Scott said.

"Do you remember the time you were eating a pear while we waited for the bus and he accused you of picking it off his tree?"

Scott grinned, his face transformed. Luke could almost see the young boy he had been. "I brought the pear from home just to mess with him. He had such a fit. He said he was going to report me to the police."

"And then on the way home from school, you came up with the idea that we should pick all his pears," she said.

"We waited until after midnight, then went

over there and picked every single pear off that tree. Then we waited at the bus stop the next morning to see what his reaction would be. He was furious! I was half afraid he'd have a heart attack, he was so stomping mad. He ran out there and started shouting about how we'd stolen all his pears." He laughed, a childish giggle. "I'll never forget the look on his face when I said, 'Do you mean all those pears on your front porch?' He turned around and there they all were, bags and bags that we'd picked and put there for him."

"He left us alone after that," Morgan said. "We made a great team, didn't we?" By this time, she was almost within striking distance of her brother. Luke tried not to focus on the sharpened blade, gleaming under the bright lights. "You know, I'm always on your side," she said. "I want to help you."

"You can't help," he said, all the joy gone from his face. "No one can."

"You have to let me try. It's in the sister handbook."

His smile was sad. "There's no such thing."

"Then maybe I ought to write one. I'll be sure to put that in."

Much of the tension had gone out of his body. "What are you going to do?"

She sat down, cross-legged, on the floor a few feet away from him. "Put down the knife and we'll both talk to some people who can help," she said. "New doctors who know about new medications. Ones that don't have the side effects you hated so much before."

"What kind of medications?"

While brother and sister talked medication and treatment options, Detective Young leaned over and whispered to Luke. "She'd make a good negotiator. She's good at defusing the situation."

"Unfortunately, she's had practice," he said.

"That's the thing about mental illness," Young

said. "All the person's family and friends become victims, too."

A clatter drew their attention. Scott had dropped the knife and risen to his feet. Morgan stood also and went to her brother and hugged him. She said something to him and he nodded, then she turned to Luke and Young. "We're ready to go to the hospital," she said.

"We've got an ambulance waiting out back," Young said.

The three of them started toward the door to the alley, where they were joined by two uniformed officers. Scott halted in the door and turned to Luke. He looked more lucid now, though still agitated. "I ran away last night because I don't like gunshots," he said. "They scared me."

"I'm sorry I upset you," Luke said. "I wasn't shooting at you."

"I saw Danny after I left here. He said if I told anybody about what I'd seen him do, he'd kill me."

"Oh, Scott." Morgan clutched at her brother's arm.

What did you see him do? Luke wanted to ask. He needed to hear the accusation against Danny in Scott's own words. But he knew he would have to wait for the answer to question the young man further. He didn't want to risk upsetting Scott again. "Thank you for telling me that," he said. But there was one question he had to ask. "Where did you see him? I can pick him up and stop him before he hurts anyone else."

Scott shook his head, his expression clouded again. "I promised not to tell. He's a bad guy. A bad guy. A bad guy…"

An EMT opened the door to the ambulance. Morgan helped Luke inside, then started to step in after him, but one of the officers motioned her aside. "We can follow in my car," Luke said, as the second officer stepped up into the ambulance.

"All right." Morgan stepped back. "I'll be there as soon as I can, Scott," she called.

Luke moved to her side. "I'll drive you to the hospital," he said.

"Are you sure? I know you have so much work to do."

"I want to make sure you're all right, first."

"I doubt you'll get to question Scott today," she said.

"I'm not concerned about Scott right now." Not really. If the young man could tell him anything useful—and that was doubtful—he'd find out soon enough. Right now, Morgan needed someone to look after her. He was making that his job.

MORGAN HUNCHED OVER the laptop, reviewing Wednesday's blog for *Cycling Pro*.

The second stage of the race brought the challenges of 8700-foot McClure Pass and 9,900-foot Kebler Pass before a steep descent into the town of Crested Butte, where crowds lined the streets to welcome racers. I spoke with US Team Amgen leader Andy Sprague by phone at the close of yesterday's race. "This is a race that starts off challenging the riders right away," he said. "But conditions have been prime so far and the fans have been incredible."

Prerace favorite Victor Vinko of Spain's Team Contador suffered a nasty crash near the top of Kebler, tangling with team member Roberto Sandoval after losing control on a rough stretch of road. No word yet on whether Vinko and Sandoval will return to the race.

At the end of Stage Two, British racer Ian McDaniel of Team Sky is the surprise leader, having pulled out a superb effort just ahead of the American peloton. The Americans hope to reclaim the yellow jersey tomorrow, when racers navigate

155 kilometers—approximately 96 miles—
between Gunnison and Monarch Mountain,
including 11,312 foot Monarch Pass, where
the weather forecast is calling for rain and
possibly snow.

She finished reading and turned to Scott,
who sat on the edge of the hospital bed, facing her. His shoulders slumped and he wore the
blank expression of someone whose emotions
were subdued under a fog of medication. But
at least he no longer trembled or raged, as he
had when they'd brought him into the psychiatric unit two days ago. "What do you think?"
she asked.

"If those guys think Kebler Pass was tough,
wait until they see Monarch this afternoon.
It's two thousand feet higher, switchback after
switchback."

"I meant about the article—though I think
you're probably right about the race. I wouldn't
even want to drive that pass, much less ride

up it on a bicycle. What do you think of Mc-Daniel's chances? You knew him in London, didn't you?"

He nodded, his expression unreadable.

She reached out and stroked his arm through the soft sweatshirt she'd brought him to wear instead of hospital scrubs. "I know you miss it," she said. "Racing." The doctors had encouraged her to talk to him about what he was feeling and experiencing. Learning to be more open about whatever was going on in his head was part of his healing.

He looked at her for so long without speaking she wondered if she'd made him angry. But finally he licked his lips and said, "I don't miss the pain or the training or the strict diet, but, yeah, I miss race days. I miss being good at something."

"You're a good photographer."

"There are a lot of good photographers out there. There aren't a lot of good racers."

She turned back to the computer. "I'm going to send this, unless you can think of something else I should add." The two of them had watched the coverage of yesterday's stage on the television in the unit's community room. Only one man had complained about their choice of television show, and an aid had escorted him to another area after a few moments.

Someone tapped on the door frame of the room and a male aide stuck his head in. "How are you this morning, Mr. Westfield?" he asked.

"I'm okay."

"You have an appointment with Dr. Chandra in the therapy room at eleven," the aide said. "We don't want to keep him waiting."

"We don't?" But Scott stood.

"I'll stop back by in about ten minutes to take you down there," the aide said, and left.

Morgan stood and began to pack away her

laptop. "I'll see you this afternoon. We'll watch the wrap-up of the third stage together."

"You don't have to spend all your time here babysitting me," Scott said.

"I want to be with you." She was still managing to get her work done while he consulted various doctors and attended therapy sessions. At night, she returned to her hotel too exhausted to worry too much about Scott's future.

"What about your boyfriend?" The smirk reminded her of the old Scott—the teasing older brother.

"He's not my boyfriend. He's just a friend."

"Right. Since when do friends make you blush like that?"

She put a hand to her hot cheek. "There's nothing between us." She had thought there might be, but she hadn't seen Luke since he'd delivered her to the hospital Tuesday evening. He'd called once while she was with Scott and left a message that he'd see her soon, but that was it. She didn't blame him for keeping his distance. Her brother's problems would scare off plenty of men, but she wasn't about to turn her back on Scott for the sake of romance. "He's very busy with work," she said.

Scott scowled. "Cop work."

"He's trying to find the person or group of people who've been setting off bombs at races," she said.

"And he thinks I had something to do with that."

"Of course not!"

"Don't lie to me. You're lousy at it." He shoved both hands into the pockets of his sweatpants. "Besides, I know the score by now. Always blame the crazy person."

"Don't say that. You're not crazy." She hated the word and all the implications that went with it.

"All right. I'm sick. Damaged."

Those words were even worse. "Sick people

can get well," she said. "Damage can be repaired. You're doing well on the new meds, aren't you?"

He shrugged. "It's only been two days."

"But you're doing well. And you'll do even better."

"Are they going to let me out of here tomorrow? It's a mandatory three-day hold, right? That's over tomorrow."

"Seventy-two hours, yes." The maximum time they could legally hold someone for psychiatric observation. After that, would Scott be free to go? No charges had been filed—she wondered if she had Luke to thank for that. "I think you should wait and hear what your doctor has to say," she said. "If he clears you for outpatient treatment you can come stay with me. Or Dad and Nicole would love to see you."

"I talked to them on the phone last night. Nicole cried. Dad sounded like he was going to."

"They've been so worried about you." She'd

called them from the hospital waiting room on Tuesday night. They'd been thrilled to hear she'd found Scott, but heartbroken to learn the circumstances and that he was back in the hospital. They'd agreed to wait and see him when he was able to travel back to Texas, trusting Morgan to take care of things in Denver.

"I don't think I could take their hovering over me," Scott said. "Like I was some toddler who was in danger of wandering out in the street. I can take care of myself."

"We'll work something out."

The scowl returned. "Little sister swooping in to save the day. Except you can't always do that."

The aide returned. "Ready for your appointment, Mr. Westfield?"

Morgan slung her laptop bag over her shoulder and kissed Scott's cheek. "I'll see you this afternoon."

"Don't feel obligated."

"I have to watch the races anyway. It's part of my job. It's more fun to watch them with you. You give me the insider's point of view."

"My opinion today is that the US team is going to take the yellow jersey again. They've got an advantage in this altitude."

"You'd make a good race analyst," she said.

"Right. People are lining up to hire me." He turned and left with the aide, but his words had sparked an idea in Morgan's head.

What if someone did hire Scott to analyze or provide commentary for bike races? As a former racer, he had the knowledge, and when he was well, he was very well-spoken and charming. It wouldn't hurt for her to call a few people she knew and talk to them. Maybe one of them would give him a tryout.

Excited by the possibilities, she hurried to her car. She was crossing the parking lot when her cell phone rang. "Ms. Westfield?" a woman's terse voice asked.

"Yes?" She shifted her laptop bag and juggled the phone and her car keys.

"This is Nurse Adkins. Could you please return to your brother's room?"

She dropped the keys, and almost dropped the phone. "Is something wrong? Is everything all right?"

"He's very agitated and he keeps asking for you."

"I'll be right there." She pocketed the phone, retrieved her keys and raced back into the hospital. What had happened to upset Scott in the few minutes since she'd left him? She pressed the up button for the elevator and waited, arms crossed, feet tapping. What was taking so long? Scott was on the ninth floor, or she would have risked the stairs.

At last, the bell dinged and the doors slid open. She had to step aside to allow an aide with a stretcher to exit, followed by an elderly man. She forced herself to be patient as he moved slowly after the stretcher, head down, taking short, shuffling steps. He took so long the elevator started to close behind him. She lunged for the door, catching it just in time and slipping inside. Then began the slow crawl upward, the car stopping on almost every floor.

When they reached the ninth floor, she burst from the car and raced for Scott's room, skidding in the door, but the sight that greeted her made her stop short.

A large male orderly and a nurse who was almost as big leaned over the hospital bed where Scott lay. He thrashed against the restraints that held him and screamed obscenities, his face twisted in rage. The nurse looked over her shoulder as Morgan entered the room. "Speak to him," she said.

Morgan moved carefully to Scott's side and raised her voice to be heard over his shouts. "Scott! It's me, Morgan! It's going to be okay. Tell me what's wrong."

He quieted and stared up at her, eyes wide with fear, straining against the straps that held him to the bed. "I saw him," he said, his voice hoarse.

"Saw who?" she asked.

He flicked his gaze to the nurse, then pressed his lips together and shook his head.

Morgan turned to the nurse, fighting back rage at seeing her brother treated like some kind of animal. "Why do you have him restrained? What happened?"

Morgan's anger didn't faze the nurse. "He was on his way to the treatment room to see Dr. Chandra and he suddenly became very agitated," she said. "He tried to run away. When Carlos tried to calm him down, Mr. Westfield took a swing at him." She turned to the med tray on the table beside the bed. "His doctor has ordered a sedative to calm him down."

Morgan suppressed a shudder at the sight of the syringe. "Let me talk to him first, please."

Not waiting for an answer, she leaned over Scott's stiff but now silent form. "What happened to upset you?" she asked, her hand on his shoulder.

"I saw him," he whispered, so softly she could scarcely make out the words.

"Saw who?"

"It was just one of the orderlies." The aide—his name tag read Carlos—spoke. "We passed him in the hall."

Her eyes met Scott's and he shook his head, though whether in denial or warning she couldn't tell.

"Which orderly?" she asked.

"One of the temps from the agency. Ricky or Rick—something like that. He walked past us, carrying a bag of dirty laundry, and your brother flipped. Started shouting that he had to get away."

"You have to get me out of here," Scott

pleaded, and began straining at his bindings once more.

"That's enough, Mr. Westfield." The nurse took hold of his arm and inserted the needle. When she finished giving the injection, her eyes met Morgan's, but there was no warmth there. "That will calm him down."

Morgan realized any protest she made at this point was useless. "May I stay with him until he goes to sleep?" she asked.

"All right." Nurse Adkins picked up the medication tray. "Leave the door open and call if you need anything."

She and Carlos left. Morgan sat on the edge of the bed and stroked Scott's hand. "They don't believe me," he said. "No one believes me."

"I believe you. Why did seeing the orderly upset you? Did he do something to hurt you earlier?"

He turned his face to the wall. "It's all right,"

she said. "You can tell me. I'll do anything I can to help you."

"It was Danny," he said.

She blinked, not sure she'd heard him correctly at first. "What did you say?"

He looked at her once more, the sedative already beginning to relax his features and slur his words. "It was Danny," he said. "He was coming to get me." Then his eyes closed, and he slipped into unconsciousness.

Chapter Seven

"Carmichael and I checked out the address where we got the tip about suspicious activity, but whoever was living there is long gone." Luke leaned back against his car, phone pressed close to his ear to shut out the sounds of passing traffic. A beep alerted him to another incoming call, but he ignored it.

"Did you talk to the neighbors? Business owners? The landlord?" Blessing barked the questions in rapid fire.

"We did. And no one knows anything. The landlord says the man he spoke to was named Smith. He paid three months' rent in advance, in cash, and he never saw him after that. The people who actually lived in the house—a woman and two men—were quiet, kept to themselves and didn't cause trouble. He thought their last name was Brown, but he wasn't sure."

"Any description?"

"Nothing we can use. According to the neighbors, both the men were average height and the woman was a little shorter. One of the men was balding. The woman was either a blonde or had light red hair, depending on who you talk to. One of the men wore glasses—sometimes. Are you sure the tip was legit?"

"They were getting mail from a contact we've been watching for a while and one of the men—whose name isn't Brown, but Brainard—visited a local machine shop and asked a lot of questions about explosives. The owner of the shop was suspicious enough to call in a report."

The incoming call alert sounded again. Probably Travis wanting to go to lunch. "Then somebody must have tipped them off, because the place is clean," he said. "And nobody saw them leave, or remembered the license plate number on their car, or took any pictures, or anything useful."

"We've got a photo of Brainard. Not a great one, but it's a place to start. I'll send it to your phone and you can show it around, see if you get any better answers. And I want you to talk to the machine shop owner, too. Maybe he's remembered something he didn't tell the local police officer who did the initial interview."

"Will do." He squinted across the parking lot toward a giant sculpture of two lanky dancers—five-story-tall modified stick figures all in white. There was an image he didn't necessarily want stuck in his head, but it would be there now, along with the faces of his suspects, who had all disappeared, the cashier at the burger place where he'd stopped for lunch, and the doorman at the hotel where he'd dropped Agent Carmichael after their fruitless search for the suspected members of a terrorist cell who'd rented the duplex in Denver's Five Points neighborhood. "Any news of our other suspect?" he asked.

"He's gone underground again. We got the autopsy back on Tuesday. Definitely cyanide poisoning. We're starting to think this might be unrelated to the bombings. Terrorists usually aim for a bigger impact. They want to take a lot of people out, not just one. This poisoning doesn't fit the pattern."

"Scott Westfield told his sister he saw Danny put something in one of the entrées waiting to go out to the dining room," Luke said.

"You should have said something before now," Blessing said. "We'll send someone to question him."

"I already tried that," Luke said. "His doctor won't hear of it until the end of his seventy-two-hour hold."

"Do you think Westfield is telling the truth? Is he making it up to get attention, or maybe to throw suspicion off himself?"

"I don't know. But I'd like the chance to question him. He's met me and I think he'd be more relaxed around me." He didn't know any such thing, but he thought it sounded plausible.

"I don't like it. Not given your relationship with his sister."

Luke stiffened. "Sir, there is no relationship." Not that he hadn't entertained the possibility, but the timing was lousy for both of them.

"Do you make a habit of kissing strangers on the street?" Blessing sounded almost amused.

Luke closed his eyes and suppressed a groan. He'd done his best to forget about that photograph. "There is no relationship," he repeated.

Again, the incoming call beep sounded. Luke ground his teeth together. *Go away*, he thought.

"I'll consider it," Blessing said. "In the meantime, see what you can get me on Brainard and company."

He ended the call and hit the symbol to check his missed calls. As he did so, the message alert popped up. *Morgan.* His heartbeat sped up when he saw her name on the screen. He punched the voice mail symbol and waited for the call to connect.

"You have one new message and three old messages," the mechanical voice intoned. "First old message…"

"Yeah, yeah, yeah." He clicked through the old messages. "First unheard message," the voice offered.

"Luke, please call me as soon as you get this message." Morgan spoke loudly, the words rushed together. "Scott saw Danny today. In the hospital. He's posing as an orderly, calling himself Rick or Ricky or something like that. Nobody believes him, but I know Scott's telling the truth. He's terrified and so am I. I'm staying with him until I hear from you."

He had his keys out and was starting the car by the time his call to Morgan connected. "Thank God, you called," she said, sounding out of breath. "The nurses made me leave Scott's room because morning visiting hours are over. I'm in a waiting room down the hall, but I can't see his room from here. Anyone could go in there. What if Danny tries to hurt him? He knows Scott saw him tampering with the food at the restaurant. What if he—?"

"Calm down. I'm on my way." He steered the car onto the street, past the giant dancers, toward the hospital where Scott was confined. "Have you contacted hospital security?"

"No. I didn't think they would believe me. The nurse and the other orderly didn't believe Scott. They think he's hallucinating or being paranoid. They wouldn't listen to me when I tried to talk to them, either."

"All right. As soon as I get off the phone with you, I'll call and talk to Security. Try to stay calm and I'll be there as soon as I can."

"All right. Thank you. Just talking to you makes me feel better."

The words pulled at something in his chest. "I'll see you soon." He ended the call, but instead of trying to find the number for hospital security, he called Special Agent in Charge Blessing. "Scott Westfield says he saw our suspect, Danny, at the hospital. The man is posing as an orderly and he threatened Westfield."

"Have you checked this out? Have you seen the orderly?"

"No, sir. I'm on my way to the hospital now."

"Luke, do I need to point out that Scott Westfield has a serious mental illness? He could be hallucinating all of this."

"He could be," Luke admitted. "But do we want to take a chance that he isn't?"

The only response for a long moment was silence. Luke pictured the team leader scowling across the desk, weighing his decision. "All right," Blessing said at last. "I'll send some men over there to check it out."

"You might alert hospital security. If they lock down the building now, we might be able to trap him."

"Do that, and we'll have the whole place in a panic. It's a hospital. If someone had a heart attack or a woman went into premature labor because they heard a terrorist was on the loose in the building, and it turns out to all be the delusion of a psychiatric patient, who do you think is going to get called on the carpet for it?"

"Sir—"

"You go down there and talk to Westfield. Assess the situation and come to me with some evidence that our suspect is there. Then I'll think about a lockdown."

"Yes, sir," he said, jaw clenched. He ended the call and took the exit for the hospital.

Inside the lobby, he headed for the reception desk. "I need to speak to hospital security," he said, and flashed his credentials. Wide-eyed, the receptionist pointed to a door behind her marked Security.

A stocky young man who didn't look to Luke as if he was old enough to order a beer looked up from behind a desk. On the wall to his right, an array of screens showed the parking lot, elevators and other areas of the hospital. "You've had a security breach in the psychiatric unit," Luke said.

"What?" The guard gaped at Luke. "Who are you? This is the first I've heard—"

"Luke Renfro, FBI." Luke showed his creds, then grabbed the guard by the arm. "Come with me. We might still have time to stop this."

The young man whose name badge read Cramer shook off Luke's hand but led the way to the elevators. He punched the button for nine, then turned to Luke. "What's this all about?"

"We have reason to believe one of the orderlies on the ninth floor is an imposter. He's a suspect, wanted for questioning in a case we're working on."

"Then why not just arrest him? Why all the drama?"

"He knows we're after him, so he's not likely to come willingly. He could be a very dangerous man."

"Huh." Cramer hooked his thumbs into his belt. "So what's he done?"

"He's threatened one of your patients, for one thing." The elevator doors opened. Luke scanned the hallway, then followed signs toward double doors. He tried the doors, but they didn't budge.

"They're kept locked," Cramer said, coming up behind him. "A nurse has to buzz you in." He pressed a button on an intercom beside the door. "Security. Open the doors, please."

A buzzer sounded and Cramer pushed open

the doors. A tall, broad-shouldered nurse in pink scrubs met them on the other side. "Mr. Cramer, what is the meaning—"

"Agent Renfro, FBI," Luke interrupted. "Where is Scott Westfield's room?"

The nurse stared at Luke's badge and ID, but her expression only hardened. "You can't see him without permission from his doctor, no matter who you are."

"Luke!" Morgan hurried past the nurse to join him. "It's all right, Nurse Adkins," she said. "Agent Renfro is here to help."

"I don't care if he's Santa Claus or Saint Francis. Morning visiting hours are over and both of you need to leave," the nurse said.

"You've had a security breach," Luke said.

"We've had no such thing," the nurse said. She turned to Cramer. "Why did you bring him up here? It's against the rules and it's disrupting our schedule."

"He's FBI!" Cramer's expression grew as

stubborn as hers. "I think that outranks either one of us."

"I'll show you where Scott's room is." Morgan took Luke's arm and pulled him down the hallway.

"You can't go in there," the nurse protested, but Luke pushed past her.

The room was a narrow cubicle with a chair, a rolling table and a hospital bed, where Scott slept on his back, his face slack. "He's sedated." Morgan smoothed the blanket over her brother's arm. "I don't know when he'll wake up."

Luke moved to her side and put his arm around her. She leaned against him, and he felt her gratitude at his presence without her having to say a word. "Tell me what happened," he said.

"I left to go back to my hotel and I hadn't even made it to my car when the nurse called to tell me Scott was freaking out. When I got here, they had him tied to the bed and were getting ready to sedate him. The aide said they'd passed an orderly in the hall and Scott freaked out. Scott told me the orderly was Danny, and that he made some kind of threat. And then the sedative took effect and he passed out."

"What did the aide say about the orderly?"

"That his name was Rick or Ricky and that he worked for a temp agency that supplies workers to the hospital. If Danny used a temp agency to get the job at the hotel, maybe he used the same ploy to get a job here. It wouldn't have been that hard to figure out that Scott was here, if he knew about the incident in the hotel kitchen and that this was where the city sends its psychiatric holds."

Luke squeezed her shoulder. "Give me a minute. I'm going to see what I can find out."

He left her and went to the nurses' station.

Nurse Adkins's expression was stern but professional. "What do you need now, Agent Renfro?"

"I need to talk to an orderly—Rick or Ricky."

Adkins looked over his shoulder and called to a passing aide. "Carlos, find Ricky and bring him here, please."

The intercom buzzed and the nurse answered the summons. "Who is it?"

"FBI. Let us in, please."

Frowning at Luke, she pressed the button to release the door. A few seconds later, Travis and Gus joined Luke at the nurses' station. "Agents Steadman and Mathers, Nurse Adkins." Luke made the introductions.

"You're beginning to worry me, gentlemen," she said. "What is going on that requires three federal agents on my floor?"

"We need to question one of your orderlies in connection with a case we're working on," Luke said.

"And we need to question Scott Westfield," Travis added.

"Mr. Westfield is sedated," she said. "Even

when he wakes up, I don't know how much you'll get out of him. He's subject to delusions."

Carlos returned to the nurses' station. "I can't find Ricky," he said.

"I can page him." Nurse Adkins reached for her phone.

"Don't do that," Luke said. "We don't want to alert him that we're looking for him. We'll spread out and search for him. Cramer, you stay here with Mr. Westfield."

"Yes, sir." Cramer looked as if he was about to salute but thought better of it.

"I'll take the first three floors," Travis said. "Luke, you search the next three. Gus, take the parking garage and the attached atrium."

They split up and Luke stopped by Scott's room first. Morgan had pulled a chair up to the bedside and was holding her brother's hand. "I've got a couple of other team members here and we're searching the hospital for Danny," he said. "Call me if you see anything suspicious while I'm gone, or if Scott wakes up."

"I will. And thank you."

"You don't have to thank me for doing my job."

"No. But thank you for believing me, and for believing Scott, and for wanting to protect him from danger."

Nurse Adkins appeared in the doorway. "If you're going to search patient rooms on this floor, I have to come with you," she said.

"Fine. Just don't get in my way."

Luke had to admit that going room to room in the psychiatric ward was unnerving. Some patients stared at him blankly. Others smiled too brightly or glared or tried to start conversations. "Mr. Renfro is a hospital inspector," Nurse Adkins explained, before he could say anything. "He's verifying we're meeting all the regulations for our certification." Her eyes dared him to deny any of this.

"That's right," he said. "Have any of you seen this man?" He showed the picture of Danny, taken from the surveillance video of the London bombing, to a group of patients gathered in the day room. "He may have been dressed as an orderly."

"I saw him this morning," one young man volunteered. "He brought my breakfast."

"Why do you want to talk to him?" a woman asked. "Has he done something wrong?"

"We need to check his vaccination records," Nurse Adkins said.

"Have any of you seen him this afternoon?" Luke asked.

They all shook their heads or murmured no. He moved on to the next room. "Vaccination records?" he asked Adkins.

"One of the state requirements is that all employees be up to date on their vaccinations and TB testing."

"Good thinking to allay suspicion," he said.

"One of my jobs is to keep everyone calm."

"Then I'd say you do a good job." They moved from room to room, questioning anyone they encountered. Most of them didn't remember any of the orderlies' names or faces. The few who did hadn't seen Ricky since breakfast.

They were almost to the last room when Luke's phone alerted him to a call from Travis. "What have you got?" Luke asked.

"I found a set of scrubs and a name badge in a stall in the men's room on the second floor," he said. "The name on the badge is Ricky. My guess is he changed into civilian clothes and left the building."

Luke swore under his breath. "I'll meet you in the security office, behind the reception desk in the ground floor lobby," he said. "We'll see if the security cameras show anything." He ended the call and turned to Nurse Adkins. "Call Security and ask them to send someone up to guard Scott Westfield. I need Cramer to meet us in his office."

"Saying please wouldn't undermine your authority, Agent Renfro."

He bit back a smile. "Point taken. Would you call Security, please?"

"I'll be happy to."

Travis met him outside the guard's room. "What are the chances Danny boy is still on the premises?" Travis asked.

"Slim to none," Luke said. "But maybe we'll get lucky and get video from the parking lot of his car or of him meeting someone."

"He hasn't slipped up yet," Travis said. "But anything can happen."

Cramer arrived and unlocked the door to the security office and led them inside. "Which cameras do you want to look at first?" he asked.

"I found the scrubs and the name tag in the men's room in the north wing of the second floor," Travis said. "Let's start there and see if we can pick him up."

"There's a camera at the end of the hall by the stairs, and one in the elevators," Cramer said.

"Start with the stairs," Luke said. "This guy is trying to keep a low profile."

Cramer sat at the desk and worked at the computer for a few moments. "How far back do you want me to go?" he asked.

"According to Morgan, her brother reported seeing Danny on the ninth floor about ten thirty," Luke said. "So go back to that time and roll forward from there."

A few moments later, a view of the door leading to the stairs on the second floor appeared on-screen. The timer on-screen showed that Cramer was fast-forwarding the video, but the view never changed. "Nothing on camera between ten thirty and now."

"Try the view of the elevator," Luke said.

A steady stream of people got on and off the

elevator—hospital personnel in scrubs, men, women and children arriving and departing in groups as they visited patients, patients in wheelchairs leaving the hospital or being taken to other floors for treatments or testing. But there was no one who looked like their suspect.

"Wait. Freeze it there." Travis pointed to the screen and Cramer stopped the video. "That guy."

Luke leaned toward the screen and studied the solitary figure who waited for the elevator. A slight male, he wore jeans, sneakers and a gray hoodie with the hood pulled over his face. "That's our man," he agreed.

"How can you tell?" Cramer asked.

"His posture," Travis said. "The set of his shoulders. It's the same as the videos we have."

"Plus, the fact that he's wearing the hoodie to hide his face. Most people don't dress that way—not to visit a friend or family member in the hospital."

"Come on, turn around." Travis spoke to the figure in the video.

The elevator doors opened and the man in the hoodie got on. "I'll switch to the feed inside the elevator," Cramer said.

The screen flickered, and then they were watching their quarry step onto the elevator. Before the doors had even finished closing behind him, the screen went white.

"What happened?" Travis asked. "Did we lose the feed?"

"The camera is still rolling." Cramer tapped the screen, where the timer showed the seconds advancing. "I think he's covered the camera with something."

"He stuck an index card over the lens," Travis said. "Put double-stick tape on one side, tape a long straw to the back. Stick it up there and when you leave, pull it off. It's easy to conceal in a pocket and as long as you're alone in the car when you put it up and take it off, no one's going to notice. If the car gets full, you can leave it in place and walk away."

"Clever," Cramer said.

"Too clever," Luke said. "Why can't we get one step ahead of this guy?"

"Switch to the ground floor, outside the elevators," Travis said. "He's got to exit there."

Again the screen filled with snow, then cleared to show the lobby elevators. The doors to the left elevator opened and the man in the hoodie emerged. He moved quickly, head down, and, in less than five seconds, disappeared from view. "Give us the exit doors," Luke said. "The ones leading to the parking lot."

"Right. That's North Seventeen. Give me a sec. Here you go."

The screen showed the double doors leading to the parking lot as people of all ages and sizes entered and exited. But no man in a gray hoodie. "It's like he disappeared," Cramer said.

Chapter Eight

"He didn't disappear." Luke rubbed his chin and continued to study the screen. "Back up the video and run it again. Half speed."

Cramer did so and they watched the flow of people toward the doors. "Freeze it!" Luke commanded. He pointed at the screen. "Now zoom in, here."

The image of a man in a white T-shirt and jeans, a red ball cap pulled over his eyes, filled the screen. "He's carrying the hoodie now," Travis said. "He must have had the cap in his pocket."

"I don't see how you recognize him as the same man," Cramer said.

"Would you recognize your mother if she walked across the screen?" Luke asked. "Even if she had her back to you and she'd changed clothes?"

"Well, sure. She's my mother."

"I know this guy's image like I know my mother's," Luke said. He hadn't asked for this particular talent, but he was going to use it to stop this guy from killing any more innocent people. "Zoom back out and let's see where he goes."

Cramer did so, switching to the parking lot surveillance when Danny moved too far from the building. But a minute later, he had moved too far for even those cameras to see him.

"He's either parked down the street, or someone is going to swing by and pick him up," Travis said.

"What's the time stamp on our last image of him?" Luke asked.

"Ten forty-seven," Cramer said.

"He didn't waste time getting out of here once Scott made him," Luke said.

"What was he doing here in the first place?" Travis asked.

"Yeah," Cramer said. "What was he doing here?"

"He knows Scott saw him in the hotel kitchen Monday night," Luke said. "It's possible he wanted to find out how much he knew."

"Or, he wanted to make sure he didn't tell anyone what he saw," Luke said.

"How did he get past our security?" Cramer asked. "Even the temp workers have to have a background check and special credentials to work on the ninth floor."

"Who checks those credentials?" Travis asked.

Cramer looked puzzled. "I don't know. Human Resources, I guess."

"So, if someone shows up on the ninth floor with an official-looking name badge and acts like he's supposed to be there, everyone assumes he's been cleared by HR," Luke said.

"I guess so," Cramer said. "But he'd still have to have an ID. You have to scan it to get in."

"He probably stole it," Travis said. "People get careless."

"Yeah, I guess enough people hate their jobs that they don't see why anyone would want to go out of their way to be here," Cramer said. "But you didn't hear that from me."

"I'll talk to Blessing, see if we can get someone over here to guard Scott Westfield and look out for Danny boy to come back."

"Danny?" Cramer asked. "I thought his name was Ricky."

"Don't worry about it." Luke put a hand on the guard's shoulder. "You've been a big help to us. I'll be sure to put in a good word with your bosses."

"Thanks. And maybe you could play up my role to Nurse Adkins."

"Adkins?" Luke tried to muffle his surprise.

"Yeah." Cramer grinned. "I've been trying to get her to go out with me. She's amazing."

Not the word Luke would have used, but there was something to be said for a tough woman. "I'll see what I can do."

He and Travis left the office and returned to the ninth floor. While Travis phoned Blessing, Luke slipped into Scott's room. Morgan jumped up from the chair beside the bed. "Did you find him?"

"No. But he's definitely out of the building." He moved to her side. "We're going to guard Scott's room until he's discharged," he said.

"So you believe he's in danger?"

"We don't want to take any chances. You should go to your hotel and try to get some rest."

"I have work I need to do. I need to watch

the results of today's stage and write my blog entry for tomorrow." She glanced at the bed. "Scott and I had planned to watch the race results together."

"Would you settle for me watching it with you instead?"

She looked into his eyes, clearly pleased with the idea. "Don't you have a lot of work to do?"

"I need to write a report, and I have some other paperwork to review." He also needed to interview neighbors around the vacant rental that may or may not have been occupied by suspected terrorists, but he could delegate some of that work to others and postpone the rest. He needed time to review the situation and ponder his next move. Chasing after Danny—pursuing without a plan every time he appeared on their radar—wasn't bringing them any closer to stopping the terrorists. He wanted to analyze the guy's behavior thus far and see if he could spot any patterns or weaknesses.

And he wanted to spend more time with Morgan, especially when she needed him, as she seemed to now.

"Then, do you want to come back to my hotel with me?" she asked. "We could order in some lunch."

"That's a great idea," he said. And he hoped that, for the next few hours at least, his suspect wouldn't set off any bombs, commit any murders or generally cause trouble.

MORGAN HADN'T REALIZED how small her hotel room was until she was alone in it with Luke. Hanging out with him all afternoon while they both worked had seemed like a good idea at the hospital. He could distract her from her worries about Scott, and maybe she could even help him with his case.

He distracted her, all right, but not necessarily in a good way. At least, not good if she was going to focus on her work. "I'll just, um, let in some more light." She crossed to the window and pulled open the drapes.

Luke picked up the room service menu from the desk. "I'm starved. What do you want to order?"

"The deli on the corner will deliver, too," she said. "They have good sandwiches and salads. Their card is by the phone."

"Sounds good." They settled on club sandwiches, fruit and bottled water. Luke ordered, while she looked for some place to set up her computer.

"They said they'll have everything up in about fifteen minutes," he said, hanging up the phone.

"That's good," she said. "You know, if you'd rather, there are some rooms off the lobby we could use, with tables and more room to spread out."

"No, this is better. More private." He unknotted his tie, then slipped off his jacket. "We can make ourselves comfortable here." He unbuttoned his shirt cuffs and began rolling up his sleeves, and she had to look away. Something about his strong, tan forearms, lightly dusted with brown hair, was doing a number on her insides. She had to fight the urge to move over to him and finish unbuttoning his shirt.

"You take the desk," she said. "I'll take the bed." She fumbled with her computer cord, her cheeks hot. "I mean, it's where I usually work." That hadn't come out well, either. "I mean, on the computer."

He chuckled, a soft, sexy sound that made more than her cheeks feel hot. "I know what you mean. The desk works fine for me." He began to unpack his laptop while she kicked off her shoes and arranged pillows against the headboard. All she had to do was pretend the sexiest man she'd ever met wasn't sitting a few feet away from her. It was just like in college when she'd had guys over to study.

A flashback to a particularly hot and heavy study session from her college years filled her mind and she quickly pushed it away. Okay, so maybe not just like in college.

She'd just opened the file with her notes from yesterday's interview with American leader Andy Sprague when a knock on the door made her jump. "That's probably our food," Luke said. He crossed to the door and she saw that he'd removed his shoes, also.

"Let me get you some cash," she said, starting to get up.

"It's okay. I'll put it on my expense account. Your tax dollars at work." He winked—actually *winked*—at her. The only other person she could ever remember winking at her was her grandpa. This was definitely not a grandpa wink.

They both fell on the food like starving people, though she didn't have any faith that a sandwich and banana were going to do much to sate the hunger that was building inside her. When the meal was reduced to crumbs, she washed her hands and returned to her computer, determined to knock out the work she needed to get done. The complete blog post would have to await the results of the day's race, but she had plenty of other work to keep her busy.

Unfortunately, the intrigues of international bike racing couldn't compete with her interest in the man at the desk across from her. In between paragraphs, she found her gaze drifting to him. His hair was tousled, as if he'd been running his hands through it, and he slouched in his chair, long legs stretched out in front of him, the relaxed pose so different from the imposing agent who had first confronted her. The man she had come to know still had that sexy, dangerous edge, but he'd also revealed his vulnerability, his frustration at failing to stop the man he was pursuing and his grief over his own missing brother. She felt connected to him in a way she hadn't felt connected to anyone else in her life—ever. The knowledge both thrilled and unsettled her.

"What are you working on?"

His question startled her from her musings. Did he realize she'd been staring at him? She shifted her gaze to her computer screen. "I'm writing up an interview I did with Andy Sprague for a sidebar to accompany the feature I'm working on for *Road Bike Magazine*, and then I need to outline my blog post for tomorrow." Feeling calmer, she risked meeting his gaze. "What about you?"

"I'm analyzing every sighting we've had of Danny—where, when, what he was wearing, what he was doing, time of day. I'm trying to spot patterns."

"Are you having any luck so far?"

"No. He's being careful. Too careful for someone working alone."

She set her laptop aside and shifted toward him. "What do you mean?"

"No one can think of every possible danger. For that you need a team. Other people who can share their experience and ideas, what they've learned, and spot potential dangers."

That made sense. "So you think he has people helping him?"

"Almost certainly. He has to have other people to provide supplies, transportation, shelter."

"Are these just minions, or people he's hired, or do you think he's part of some organized group?"

"He could be part of a terrorist cell."

The words were straight out of a thriller novel or a spy movie. Sure, she'd read plenty of news stories about terrorism, but she still had a hard time wrapping her mind around the idea of terrorists living, working and organizing in this country. The knowledge made her realize how important the work of people like Luke really was. She moved to the end of the bed and studied the spreadsheet he'd pulled up on the screen.

"You realize this is all highly classified and I'm breaking all kinds of rules letting you see it." His voice was gentle, but all the same, he pressed a button to close the screen.

She could have complained that he didn't trust her but, honestly, in his job, how could he afford to trust anyone? And she had to give him points for telling her as much as he had. Better to make light of the moment. "I promise I'm not an enemy spy trying to seduce all your secrets from you," she said.

"Too bad." He moved his chair so that he was positioned directly in front of her, his knees bumping the end of the bed. "If anyone could distract me from my duty, it might be you."

"Could I distract you like this?" Tentatively— just in case she'd read him wrong—she leaned forward and pressed her lips to his. His arm came around her, steadying her and deepening the kiss. The sweep of his tongue across her lips made every nerve tingle and glow, and all thoughts of caution deserted her. All she wanted was for this kiss, this moment, to never end.

He was the first to pull away, although reluctantly. He traced the line of her jaw with one finger, his gaze searching. "There's nothing I'd like better than to turn off my phone and take you to bed right now," he said. "But I think we both know that wouldn't be a good idea."

"Because my brother is a suspect in your case." Saying the words made her feel cold. She withdrew her arms from around him and hugged herself.

"Not a suspect. But someone who might have important information that could help us."

"So you can't afford to get involved with me."

He caressed her shoulder. "If I was anyone else, in any other job, we wouldn't be having this conversation. We'd already be making love. But I'm not someone else, and, because of my job, I have to think about not only the circumstances that surround us now, but how those circumstances are going to look in a court case later. A defense attorney might be able to use an affair between us to discredit my testimony or your brother's, or to distract the jury from the important issues of the case. I've seen it happen before."

She nodded. How many times had she seen political campaigns derailed by personal issues or sexy stories trump real news in the headlines? "You're right." She sat back but couldn't resist giving him her most seductive smile. "But I'm warning you right now, when this case is over…"

"I'll be putting in for a long vacation. With you."

She laughed, though the heat of unrequited lust still simmered between them. Checking the clock, she was surprised to see it was almost two. "The race coverage started at one thirty," she said. "I try to catch as much of it as I can."

He handed her the remote. "Mind if I watch it with you?"

"Of course not." She switched on the TV and scooted back on the bed.

He moved his chair around to face the screen. "What is it you like about bike racing?" he asked. "I admit, I don't know much about it."

"I didn't, either, until Scott started racing. I got to know other riders and saw how hard they all worked and trained. The races themselves are grueling for the racers, but exciting, too. They're fast paced and there's a lot of strategy that goes into the races. It's both an individual and a team event. One racer may win a stage or a race, but he relies on his team to help him."

"Your brother must miss it."

"He does. He was very good at racing. When

he had to leave it, he lost his focus. And he'd been in racing so long all his friends were there. I think he misses being part of that family. I've tried to encourage him to find new interests and make new friends, but he says it's too hard."

The screen switched to a close-up shot of the racers, straining to make the grueling climb up a mountain pass. The camera panned over the crowds of fans who lined the course, some holding signs, others waving flags. Luke leaned forward, his gaze focused on the television.

Morgan found herself watching him instead of the racers. "You're doing it now, aren't you?" she asked.

"Doing what?" His gaze remained fixed on the screen.

"You're looking for people you recognize from the other races."

"I'm looking for someone I recognize who is acting suspicious or seems out of place," he said. "Other members of the team are along the course. They're looking for any of our suspects, too."

"What happens if they spot someone?"

"They request that he—so far all our suspects are male—will come in to answer some questions."

"What if the person refuses to come?"

"Almost everyone does. We're good at giving the impression we won't take no for an answer."

"Yes. You definitely gave me that impression."

The television switched to a commercial and he turned to her, his expression grave. "I'm not in the habit of using my position to pick up women," he said. "I want you to know that."

"Then why did you follow me that day?"

"Partly because I was attracted to you, and I wanted to know more about you."

"And the other part?"

"I had a feeling. Call it instinct, or a hunch.

After a while in this job, you learn not to ignore those feelings."

"Are you sure you aren't trying to justify your actions? Not that I'm complaining, mind you."

"Maybe I am. But finding you also led me to your brother, and I still think he could be an important link in this case."

Scott again. Would he always be a barrier between them? "Luke, no! I realize Scott has had his share of problems, and you probably think because he's lonely and drifting he'd be susceptible to people who pretend to be his friends, but Scott isn't that naive. He wouldn't be taken in by terrorists, and he wouldn't hurt innocent people." Her voice broke, and she turned away, not wanting him to see the tears that burned in her eyes.

"Hey." He moved from the chair to the bed and pulled her close. "I'm not accusing Scott of being a terrorist," he said. "But I believe he knows more than he's been able to tell us. More about Danny. He could be the one who helps us break this case."

"I hope he is," she said. "I want you to capture the people responsible for all these deaths, but I also want Scott to have something positive in his life. I want him to see that his diagnosis and having to give up racing don't have to be the end."

"Then I hope I can help him see that."

He kissed her temple, a gesture of tenderness and comfort. But she needed more from him. Not everything she wanted—at least not now—but a reminder of what might one day be between them.

She turned toward him, her lips angled to his. "Kiss me," she whispered.

She closed her eyes and surrendered to the storm of emotions his kiss stirred within her— passion and tenderness, wonder and worry. She wanted her feelings for this man—the connection she felt for him—to be real. But could she trust herself to love when so many other things battled for her attention? Was she drawn to Luke because he offered respite from the storm or because he was the person she was meant to be with, someone who was proving already that he would stand by her for better or worse?

A loud ringing jolted them apart. "My phone," he said, scowling toward the sound, which came from the jacket he'd hung on the back of the desk chair.

"You'd better answer it." She sat back against the headboard, trying to control her breathing and slow her racing heart.

He snagged the jacket from the chair, then extracted the phone. "Agent Renfro," he answered, his voice crisp and professional.

He listened for a moment, the twin lines between his eyes deepening. Then he hung up, stood and began shrugging into his jacket.

"What is it?" she asked. "What's wrong?"

"We need to go," he said, and began to shut down his computer. "That was the hospital. Your brother has disappeared."

Chapter Nine

Luke reached the hospital before Morgan and was grateful for a few moments to take stock of the situation before she arrived. Travis met him at the ninth-floor elevator. "What happened?" Luke asked.

"Another patient had what is politely known as an episode. He attacked a nurse and the officer assigned to guard Scott went to her aid. When he came back, Westfield's room was empty."

"Have you checked security footage?"

"Gus is reviewing it now. Did you notify the sister?"

"She's on her way." He and Morgan had agreed that coming in separate vehicles was less likely to arouse suspicion.

He followed Luke to Scott's hospital room. They had to squeeze past Carlos, who was righting an overturned cart, gathering up scattered syringes and meds. "You missed all the excitement, Agent Renfro," he said.

"What set off the patient?" Luke asked.

Carlos shrugged. "Who knows? They told me when I was assigned to this floor that I'd like the variety. I didn't realize they meant we can never really predict what these patients are going to do."

In Scott's room, the bedcovers were thrown back, restraints were discarded on the floor and IV tubing dangled from a stand by the bed. "Was he still unconscious when the officer left him?" Luke asked.

"He said Westfield was a little restless, as if he was starting to come out of sedation."

"The sedative his doctor ordered was a mild one." Nurse Adkins stood in the doorway of the room. She had a stain on the front of her scrubs and a strand of hair had come loose from the bun at the back of her head. She looked much less intimidating than she had before.

"How long should that have put him out?" Luke asked.

"It's difficult to say," she said. "But these patients sometimes develop tolerances. Adrenaline, other drugs in their system and the way their bodies process medication can result in an increased or decreased effect in their systems."

"So Scott could have been coming out of sedation already?" Luke asked.

"Yes."

"Have any strangers been on the floor in the last hour?" Travis asked. "Did the temp service send over a new orderly to replace Ricky?"

She shook her head. "No one's been allowed on the floor."

"Someone could have slipped in while everyone was distracted by the other patient," Travis said.

The sound of someone running in the hallway made them all look toward the door. Morgan burst into the room, breathless. "Have you found him?" she asked. "Do you know what happened?"

"We haven't determined that yet." Luke touched her shoulder lightly, then moved away. He needed to distract her from her panic, get her focused on something active and useful. "Tell me if you notice anything missing from this room."

She scanned the bedside table, then walked to the small wooden cabinet on the wall and opened it. "His clothes are gone," she said. "The tennis shoes and T-shirt and pants he was wearing when they brought him here."

"His medication is missing, also." Nurse Adkins pointed to the top shelf of the closet.

"The prescription was filled in anticipation of his release."

"So if someone did kidnap him, they took the time to get him dressed and to gather up his meds?" Travis shook his head. "I don't see how there was time for that."

"Let's check the surveillance tapes." Luke led the way to the elevator, followed by Travis and Morgan.

"Ms. Westfield, you need to stay here and let us handle this," Travis said.

"Let her come with us," Luke said. "Maybe she'll notice something we don't."

"Luke." The one word held a warning. Next would come the lecture about not letting personal relationships interfere with the job.

"She's his sister," Luke said. "She might be able to help."

Travis pressed his lips together but made no further objection. The three of them boarded the elevator and Luke pressed the button for the first floor. He glanced up at the camera. Its lens was uncovered, the green light on the front indicating they were being recorded. What had happened to Scott Westfield? Even if Danny had dared to return, how would he have gotten a reluctant, half-conscious or completely unconscious man out of here without someone noticing?

They found Cramer and Gus in the security office. Gus glanced up when they entered. "We've got him on tape," he said.

They crowded around the desk and Cramer worked the controls until an image of Scott filled the screen. Dressed in sweatpants and shirt, he carried a plastic bag and opened the door to the stairwell. "His other clothes were in a bag like that," Morgan said.

Cramer manipulated the controls, moving from camera to camera, following Scott down the stairs. He slipped into a bathroom on the third floor and changed into jeans and a T-shirt, then continued down the stairs and out a side door. The last image showed him at the edge of the parking lot, headed toward the street.

"How did he untie himself and get out of that bed?" Travis asked.

"Once he was unconscious, the nurse would have removed the restraints," Cramer said. "There are laws against keeping people confined for too long. They're supposed to keep people from hurting themselves or others in the short term, until they're under control."

Luke turned to Morgan. "Why did he leave?"

"Probably because he was scared," she said. "Seeing Danny really freaked him out. Once he woke up, he was probably worried Danny would come back. So he waited until the guard was gone and slipped out. He'd rather be on his own than trust the hospital."

"Where would he go?" Travis asked.

She shook her head. "I don't know. No one at the hotel where he was working could tell me where he lived." She stilled, then looked at him, her face more alert, almost hopeful, even. "I gave him my business card, with the name and address of my hotel on it. Maybe he went there."

"Go back there now and let us know the minute you see him," Luke said. "We need to talk to him and find out why he's so afraid of Danny, and what he knows that might help us."

She nodded. "Yes. I promise I'll call you as soon as I see him." She started to turn away, then looked back at Luke. "Thanks," she said. "For everything." Then she raced away, her shoes slapping on the tile lobby floor as she headed for the parking lot.

"I'll set someone to watch her hotel," Travis said, pulling out his phone. "Do you think he'll really show up there?"

"I don't know. They were close, but he's avoided her for the past year, so I'm not sure he'd have a change of heart now."

"Maybe he didn't run away to avoid Danny, but to join up with him," Travis said. "Maybe even to warn him of our suspicions."

"Danny already knows we suspect him. Even if he and Scott were partners at one time, Scott would be too much of a risk for him now. He's too unpredictable."

"Then Westfield is in danger either way you look at it."

"I hope we find him—or Danny—before we have another death on our hands." He didn't want to even think about the possibility of having to tell Morgan he hadn't been able to protect her brother. "Any news from the race?"

"An American won today's stage—Sprague? No sign of any of our other suspects. No sign of suspicious activity. If he's sticking to his pattern, he's waiting for the finale, when the biggest crowds and the greatest number of media eyes will be on the finish line."

"But he has to know there will be incredible security at the finish line," Cramer said. "I read in the paper they're installing scanners and the place will be crawling with cops and bomb-sniffing dogs."

"Some people see that kind of thing as more of a challenge," Travis said. "A call for them to up their game."

He and Luke left the office. "Now that we know Scott has left, I don't see any sense in staying here," Luke said.

"The hospital is in high security mode in case our suspect comes back, but that doesn't seem likely," Travis agreed. "We've put out an APB on Scott, so maybe one of the locals will pick him up."

"Soon, I hope," Luke said. "I think he knows more than he's telling us about our suspect."

"Did you get any information out of the sister when you went to her hotel room?"

Luke stiffened. "How did you know I went to her hotel room?"

"I might have overheard your conversation."

"I didn't go there to question her. She's not a suspect." He looked away, afraid he might reveal just how close he had become to Morgan in the short time they'd known each other.

"Until we solve this thing, everyone is a suspect." Travis spoke softly, but his voice was intense. "Even if she's not directly involved, her brother may be wrapped up in this some way. Don't compromise this case for the sake of your hormones."

"I won't compromise the case." What he felt for Morgan may have started out as pure physical attraction but went beyond that now.

Travis gripped his shoulder. "I shouldn't have said that. You're one of the best agents I know. But you know as well as I do that some people are very good liars. I'd hate to see you taken in."

He relaxed a little. "Morgan isn't lying." He started to add that Morgan wasn't like Travis's ex-fiancée, who had blindsided him when she broke off their engagement six months before. He didn't want to remind his friend of that hurt, though he knew it must be the worry behind Travis's warning to him. "But I'm still being careful. My focus right now has to be on the case."

"I'll keep you posted on this end of things," Travis said. "Where are you headed now?"

"I'm still trying to track down any leads on the suspected terrorists in that rental house in Five Points."

"Good luck."

"Thanks." They were all going to need a lot of luck to crack this case. For all the resources the Bureau was devoting to stopping these people, they kept slipping through their fingers.

MORGAN PACED HER hotel room—nine steps to the window, turn, nine steps back to the door. She stared at the cell phone in her hand, willing it to ring. She'd tried Scott's cell at least a dozen times last night before finally crawling into bed for a fitful night of half dozing and terrifying dreams in which Scott was in danger and she was unable to reach him.

This morning she'd fortified herself with coffee from room service and resumed her vigil again. All her calls had gone straight to voice mail. The thought of him out there alone, running scared through the city, made her too sad and jittery to sit down.

She turned to the television, where a local sports channel was showing live coverage of that day's race stage in Colorado Springs. Today's course was a circuit around the city, including a loop around the scenic Garden of the Gods. Apparently, one of the American team had just crashed into a fan who had stepped into the road to take a picture on his phone. Such accidents were becoming all too common at races these days. Race officials tried to publicize the dangers and urge people to stay back, but a long tradition of allowing crowds to get close to the racers made authorities reluctant to set up barricades.

The first jaunty notes of her ring tone sounded, and she yelped and hurried to answer the call.

"Hello," Luke said. "How are you doing?"

He'd called last night to check on her and reassure her, as well. Hearing from him made her feel less alone in all of this. "I'm going a little crazy, waiting and worrying." She sat on the end of the bed, shoving aside her laptop to make room. The hours she'd spent yesterday with Luke in this room had been such a sweet, welcome interlude from the worry and frustration, but now she struggled with guilt. If she had stayed at the hospital with Scott instead of returning here with Luke, could she have prevented her brother from running away?

"We're circulating Scott's picture to authorities," Luke said. "If anyone spots him, we'll hear about it."

"I checked with my dad and stepmom. They haven't heard anything." She hadn't shared that Scott might be in danger—telling them their son had disappeared again had been painful enough.

"The hotel where he worked hasn't heard anything, either," Luke said. "The address he gave them when he applied for the job is a men's shelter. They haven't seen him in three or four days."

"What is that address?" She reached for the notepad and pen by the phone. "Maybe I could talk to people there who knew him." Anything was better than sitting here doing nothing.

"Our people already interviewed everyone there." His voice softened. "I know you want to help, but the best thing really is to stay at the hotel and wait for Scott. We still think he might try to reach you."

"I hope so." Reluctantly, she set the paper and pen aside.

"Did he have a car, or credit cards?"

"I don't think so. He always rode his bike everywhere or used public transportation." When he was well, he was proud of not being tied to a car. "As for credit cards, if he was living in a shelter, working odd jobs, I doubt if he had much money."

"It was a long shot, but I had to check."

"I appreciate all you're doing." She knew he wanted to talk to Scott as a witness in his case, but she liked to believe at least part of the reason he was working so hard to find him was because of her.

"What are you doing besides worrying?" Luke asked.

"I'm watching the race coverage." She glanced at the TV, where a reporter stood on the side of the road, surrounded by a crowd of exuberant race fans. "I'll finish my blog post for tomorrow later. What are you doing?"

"I'm following some leads in another part of the case. I'm going to be pretty busy for the next day or so, so I may not get to see you, but hang in there. And try not to worry. Your brother has been doing a good job of looking after himself for the past year."

"You're right. That's a good thing for me to remember." Scott was an adult, and when he was healthy, he was smart and savvy. It was his illness that made things so unpredictable.

They said their goodbyes and she moved her laptop to the desk and turned up the volume on the television. American racer Andrew Sprague had won the race's third stage the day before, just as Scott had predicted, with an impressive performance on the mountain passes that had blown away his closest competition. She watched the replay of an interview with Sprague at the finish line yesterday. The handsome racer in the yellow jersey had the same dazzling smile and charming manner she remembered from her previous encounters with him. He'd been one of Scott's chief rivals earlier in their careers. In Scott's last race, he had beat out Sprague by less than a second. The memory of that day was etched in her mind, a permanent image of Scott, in his racing jersey, lean and muscular, drenched in the champagne his teammates had sprayed over him in their victory celebration. He'd been so happy.

Two months later, he'd received the diagnosis that ended his career. At first, he'd brought the same determination that had allowed him to win races to his battle against his mental illness. But he was fighting an elusive enemy, one that tortured his mind, while the medications to control it tortured his body. She'd watched, helpless, as he sank further into despair. And then he was gone, vanishing from her life. Knowing he was alive, somewhere, but that she was unable to reach him, was worse in some ways than losing him to death.

She pushed the thoughts away and forced herself to write the blog post that was due tonight. Losing her job wouldn't help Scott any.

An hour later, she'd finished the article and was thinking about ordering in something to eat when her cell phone rang. Heart pounding, she studied the unfamiliar number on the screen, then hurried to answer it. "Hello?"

"It's Scott. Are you alone?"

"Yes. I'm alone in my hotel room." She tried to sound calmer than she felt, fearful of scaring him away if she acted too anxious. "Where are you? Are you okay?"

"I'm fine. I know you're worried about me, but don't. I'll be okay."

"Where are you? I can come get you. Why did you leave the hospital?" She couldn't keep back the flood of questions.

"It wasn't safe there. I had to get away. It'll be better now."

"Why wasn't it safe? Tell me where you are. Let me help you, please."

"You can't help me," he said. But the words didn't hold the despair she'd heard from him before. He seemed to be calmly stating fact. "You have to look after yourself."

"I can help you," she insisted. "If nothing else, at least we can be together. Please tell me where you are."

"I can't do that. It isn't safe."

"Who is trying to hurt you? Who are you afraid of?"

"You've got it all wrong," he said. "I'm not afraid for myself. But I have to stay away, to protect you."

"Me? Scott, please—I don't understand."

"Just—look out for yourself. Stay close to your cop friend."

"Scott, let me—" But he'd ended the call.

With shaking hands, she hit the redial button. The phone rang and rang. "Come on, Scott. Answer me."

After a dozen rings a mechanical voice came on the line. "The party you are trying to reach is unavailable or out of service…"

She hung up and sat on the edge of the bed, replaying the conversation over and over in her mind. The Scott she'd spoken with just now had sounded strong and sure of himself—more like the old Scott, before his disappearance, and before his diagnosis, even. Though in recent years she'd slipped into the role of worrying about and taking care of him, when they were growing up he was the one who had protected and looked after her. If she was bullied at school, he dealt with the culprits. He vetted her boyfriends, helped her study for difficult tests, and was always there to offer advice and encouragement. She hadn't let herself think, until now, about how much she'd missed that side of her brother.

Believing she was in danger, he'd slipped back into the role of her protector. But why would he believe anyone would want to hurt her? She hadn't had any contact with Danny or anyone else associated with the bombings. How could she be in any danger?

Chapter Ten

Luke was sure half a dozen pairs of eyes watched him as he approached the last house on the street. He'd spent the morning going door to door in the neighborhood, showing pictures of their suspected terrorists and asking if anyone knew them or knew where they went. The work was simple but filled with tension. Everything about him, from his car with government plates to his suit, pegged him as a fed. Every time he knocked on a door, he braced himself for a less-than-friendly reception. Agents had been gunned down for asking questions in the wrong neighborhoods.

But today's search had yielded nothing more than wary looks and denials that anyone knew anything about the former residents of the little white house on the corner. A few people would admit to having seen one or more of them or their car, but, as one woman put it, "they kept to themselves."

A young woman with a baby on her hip and a toddler clinging to her leg answered the door at the last house. She studied Luke's credentials with wide eyes and nodded when he showed the photographs. "I know who they are, but I don't know anything about them."

"So you never spoke to them, made conversation in passing or anything like that?" he asked.

"Why are you looking for them?"

It wasn't the first time he'd been asked that question. "We think they witnessed a crime we're investigating," he said. "Finding them could help us locate a murderer."

The word "murderer" invariably got people's

attention. The young woman studied the photos again. "I talked to the woman once. She told me my little girl was pretty." She put a hand on the head of the toddler at her side. "She had kind of a Southern accent. Maybe from Georgia or someplace like that."

It wasn't much to go on, but it was something. "Was this at her house?" Luke asked.

"No. At the Gas N Go a block over. I get milk for the kids there a lot, because they put it on sale all the time, and I used to see one or all three of them in there a lot. I was buying milk and juice in there one afternoon and the woman was there. I smiled and said hello and she smiled back and said, 'Your little girl is so pretty. I always smile when I see her.'"

"What was she doing in the store?"

"I think she was buying a money card. You know, one of those credit card type things you can put cash on and send as a gift or something like that."

"Anything else you remember?"

The woman shook her head. "I think they moved out not too long after that. At least, when I walked by the house a week later, it looked empty."

"Thanks." Luke replaced the photos in his jacket and handed the woman one of his cards. "You've been a big help."

He drove to the Gas N Go and parked at the side of the building. It was a typical neighborhood convenience store, with gas pumps out front and groceries, snacks, lottery tickets, gift cards and cigarettes for sale inside. This time of the afternoon, business was brisk. Luke waited until one of the two clerks on duty wasn't busy and approached the counter.

He identified himself and showed the photos to the clerk, a middle-aged African American man with a shaved head and a paunch, whose name tag identified him as Isaiah. "Yeah, they came in here pretty regular," Isaiah said.

"What did they buy?" Luke asked.

The clerk scratched the side of his face. "Well, you know, the usual. Cigarettes, soda, chips. Sometimes they bought calling cards, which seemed a little odd, I guess."

"Why was that odd?"

"Mostly we sell those to people who want to make calls overseas. Maybe they got a kid in the military, or they want to call home to Mexico or India or wherever. These three didn't look old enough to have kids in the service and they didn't strike me as foreign."

"Anything else?"

"They bought cash cards, sometimes, those MoneyGram things. You can put up to a thousand bucks on one. The woman mostly did that. She always bought the maximum amount on each card and paid cash."

"That didn't strike you as unusual?"

"It's none of my business how people spend their money or where they get it," he said.

Isaiah wore that closed-up look that told Luke he wasn't going to get anything else out of him, so Luke got his contact information and turned toward the other clerk, who was selling lottery tickets to a young couple.

"He can't help you any," Isaiah said. "He's only been working here three days."

The other clerk, Ray, shook his head and looked puzzled when Luke showed him the pictures of the three suspects. "Sorry, I can't help you," he said. Isaiah looked on, arms crossed, his eyes sending a clear message of *I told you so*.

Luke thanked them and started to leave, but on impulse, he took out his phone and pulled up the photo of Danny.

"Do either of you recognize this man?" he asked.

They leaned in to study the photo. Isaiah nodded. "Yeah. He came in with the other three one day."

"You're sure?" Luke tried not to let his excitement show.

"I'm sure. He wore a Boston Red Sox cap and I'm a Sox fan, so I said something about it, but he blew me off."

"Anything else you can tell me about him?" Luke asked.

"His friends called him Dan."

"Dan? You're sure?"

"I'm sure. Nothing wrong with my hearing."

"Any last name?"

"I never heard one. He didn't say much, you know."

"Did you know the names of any of the others?"

"No. They never said. At least, not while I was listening."

"Thanks. You've been very helpful."

"Why are you looking for these people?" Isaiah asked. "Is there a reward if I help find them?"

Luke handed the man one of his cards. "Call me if any of them comes in here again, or if you see them around. There just might be a reward."

Back in the car, he phoned Blessing to update him on his progress. "The woman had a Southern accent, maybe Georgia, and the clerk identified our bombing suspect as having been in the store with the three from the house at least once. He says he heard one of them call him Dan."

"It's not much, but it helps us start to build a profile," Blessing said. "Anything else?"

"The clerk said Dan wore a Boston Red Sox cap."

"A Sox fan named Dan. How many of those do you think there are?"

"I'll keep digging," Luke said, and ended the call.

Immediately, his phone beeped, alerting him that he had a voice mail. He clicked over to his mailbox and Morgan's voice, thin and shaky, said, "Scott called me. He said he's okay, but that I might be in danger. What is he talking about? Luke, I'm a little scared."

He started the car and hit the button to return the call. As he peeled out of the parking lot, she answered. "Luke, thanks for calling me back," she said. "Maybe I'm worrying over nothing, but…"

"It's okay," he said. "I'm on my way."

SCOTT FOLLOWED THE faint trail along the creek bank that led to the little clearing in the underbrush where he and Danny had been camping. Well, Danny had been camping there—he'd just let Scott spread his bedroll under the trees nearby and share the campfire for a couple of nights. The men's shelter wasn't bad, but he liked being out in the woods. It reminded him a little of the church camp he'd attended for a few summers when he was a kid.

Danny had been really friendly at first. He'd remembered Scott from London and he was the first person Scott had met in a long time who wanted to talk about cycling. Danny was a real fan. He knew the names of all the top racers and had watched a lot of the big races. But he'd never been to Colorado before, so he was eager for Scott to fill him in on details about the Colorado Cycling Challenge. It felt so good to sit with a friend and talk like that. Scott wasn't a weird crazy or even a has-been who couldn't cut it. He was a veteran racer who knew the sport and was happy to share his knowledge with someone who was interested.

But something had definitely changed back there in the hotel kitchen. Danny had been doing something with the food and he'd been angry when he'd caught Scott watching him. And then he'd pulled that gun and shot at Morgan and her friend... Remembering the gun made his stomach knot. What if Danny had the gun with him now? What if he decided to kill Scott?

He froze, wondering whether he should leave while he still had the chance. He'd stay away from Danny and avoid trouble.

But he couldn't get the way Danny had looked in the hospital out of his head. Disguised as an orderly that way. Worse, Scott couldn't forget what he'd said. When they'd passed in the hall, Danny had leaned over and whispered, "Keep quiet or I'm going to hurt your sister." The way he'd said that word—*hurt*—and the look in his eyes, sent a wave of panic washing through Scott, ice flooding his veins. It was as if one of the devils in his head had come to life and was standing before him, right there in the hospital hallway.

Scott was calmer now, and he was tired of being afraid. No person could be as bad as the devils in his head. The new medicine they'd given him at the hospital had shut up those devils, and he was feeling better. Stronger. But that might not last. He had to deal with Danny now.

He'd thought about this all last night and this morning, while he hid at various spots around the city. He and Danny had been friends. Scott could talk to him. He'd let Danny know that he knew how to keep his mouth shut—he didn't rat out his friends. But Danny had to leave Morgan alone. She had nothing to do with any of this.

He started forward again, moving slowly and quietly, damp leaves on the trail muffling his footsteps. He stopped at the edge of the clearing and waited, watching and listening. Danny's tent was there, on the other side of the clearing, camouflaged by the pine boughs he'd cut and draped over it. Behind that, more pine boughs covered the black metal footlocker. When Scott had asked about the footlocker, Danny said he used it for supplies, so the animals wouldn't get to them. A heavy lock on the front of the chest kept anyone else from looking inside. Once, when Scott had sat on the foot-locker, Danny had yelled at him to stay away.

That was cool. Some guys were very partic-ular about their things. And Danny had a lot of things—backpacks and a folding table and chairs, water jugs and pots and pans and lots of canned food. How did he get all that stuff here on foot? Someone must have given him a ride. The locker was really heavy—too heavy for one person to move.

When he was certain no one was around, Scott moved closer to the tent. It was zipped up tight. He checked the locker—still locked. The ashes in the rock-lined fire ring were cold. Danny had either left early that morning, or he'd spent the night somewhere else.

Scott looked at the tent again. What if Danny was in there now, asleep? What if he was sick? Or even dead? He rubbed his hand up and down his thigh, debating what to do. Maybe he should go inside the tent and check. If Danny wasn't there, he could leave him a note.

Heart pounding so hard it hurt, he crept to the tent and eased open the zipper. He let out a rush of breath when he saw the tent was empty. The sleeping bag was neatly rolled and tied to one side, and a backpack leaned against it.

A new backpack—not the one Danny had had before. Scott squatted in front of it and unfastened the top flap. Maybe the gun was in here. If he found it, he'd take it away and throw it in the creek so that Danny couldn't use it to hurt Morgan.

In the top of the pack, he found a map of the race route, and a program with the racers' bios and pictures, as well as lots of stuff about the history of the race. Scott stared at the brochures and began to get a queasy feeling in his stomach. The medicine he took sometimes made him feel sick, but this was a different kind of sickness. Danny had asked him a lot of questions about the race. He wanted to know the best place to stand at the end of the race, where the most people would be, where the cameras were. Something about those questions wasn't right.

"What the hell do you think you're doing?"

The harsh words made Scott jump away from the pack. He recognized the voice as Danny's, but all he could focus on was the gun pointed at him.

"What are you doing going through my things?" Danny demanded.

"I…I was looking for piece of paper to leave you a note," Scott said.

"Why aren't you in the hospital? Who have you been talking to? Who have you told about this place?" Danny fired the questions like bullets, sharp and rapid. Scott searched for answers.

"I haven't been talking to anyone," he said. "I didn't tell anyone anything. I left the hospital because…because I'm fine now. I don't need to be there anymore." He forced a smile, though it felt more like a grimace. "Now that I'm out, I thought we could hang together for a while. Maybe watch the race together. I could introduce you to some racers at the finish line."

Danny ignored the invitation. He jabbed the gun toward Scott. "Who was that man in the hotel kitchen? The one with your sister?"

"How did you know she was my sister?" Scott hadn't introduced them. Morgan hadn't said anything about knowing him.

"I make it my business to know things. Who was he?"

"Some guy she's dating. I don't know his name."

"You told her about me, didn't you? I saw her there in your hospital room. The two of you looked real close."

"I didn't tell her anything." He forgot about

smiling. "She doesn't know anything. You need to leave her alone."

"Maybe I'll shut you both up," he said. "I'll kill you now, then kill her. I won't have to worry about either one of you saying anything you shouldn't."

What could Scott possibly say to that? He looked frantically around the tent for anything he could use as a weapon. Sleeping bag, back-pack, clothes—everything was too soft and lightweight to stop a gun.

"Get outside." Danny gestured with the gun. "I'm not going to shoot you in my tent, get your blood all over my stuff."

Scott debated refusing to move, but he didn't think that ploy would work. Danny would only get more angry, and might decide to shoot him anyway. He had started to crawl toward the door of the tent when the alarm on his phone sounded, the ascending and descending elec-tronic notes overly loud in the enclosed space.

"What's that?" Danny asked.

It was the reminder he'd set to take his medication, but Danny didn't need to know that. "Um, it's a text. Probably from my sister. I'm supposed to meet her for lunch. Her and her boyfriend—the cop."

Danny swore. "I knew he was a cop. Get out of the tent. Now!"

He backed away, the gun still fixed on Scott, who had to crawl through the door of the tent, then stand. "Over there, against those trees," Danny directed him.

Scott started toward the trees, but Danny put out a hand. "First, give me your phone."

Trying to control the shaking of his hand, Scott dug the phone from the pocket of his jeans and handed it over. Danny dropped it to the ground and stomped on it, grinding his heel into the screen. Then he kicked the pieces away. Scott swallowed against the nausea that climbed his throat.

"Get over there," Danny motioned to the trees once more.

A movie Scott had seen a long time ago came into his mind. A man—a detective or some other good guy—held at gunpoint by a villain. He threw gravel in the shooter's face and got away. Would that really work, or did that kind of thing only happen in the movies? If he failed, Danny would shoot him. He stared at the gun, fighting fear and paralysis. If he didn't try something, Danny was going to shoot him anyway. At least this way, he would die fighting.

He lunged forward, letting himself fall, bracing his arms to catch himself. His hand landed in the fire ring. Grabbing a handful of gravel, cinders and old coals, he flung the mess into Danny's face. The gun went off, the sound muffled, a single *pop!*

Scott didn't know if he'd been hit. He was up and running, terror propelling him back along the trail and up toward the highway on the other side of the creek. He splashed through the water and clambered up the slope, shots exploding in the dirt around him. All those years of cycling, of working out, had given him strong legs. He was fast. And he wasn't going to let this guy kill him.

He burst onto the shoulder of the freeway and didn't stop, running onto the pavement, hands in the air, screaming as loudly as he could, "Help me!" Horns blared and cars swerved around him. He reached the median and turned to look back.

Danny stood at the top of the slope, the gun nowhere in sight. He bent and picked up something off the ground. Something white, like a business card. He read it and stuffed it in his pocket, then looked up at Scott and smiled— a smile like the devils in his head wore when they looked out of his eyes into the mirror sometimes. A smile full of evil and loathing, and Scott began to be afraid all over again.

Chapter Eleven

Luke told himself he was going to Morgan's hotel to calm her down, but when she opened her door and moved into his arms, he realized how worried he'd been. "Thank you for coming," she said. "Scott sounded so certain when he said I was in danger—it really frightened me."

"Did he say why he thought that?" Luke asked, after he'd followed her inside and locked the door behind them. "Has someone threatened you?"

"He said he had to stay away to protect me. I thought maybe he was talking about Danny—

that Danny was after him and he was afraid to involve me." She sat on the edge of the bed, hands clasped tightly in her lap. "I don't know what to think."

"How did he sound on the phone?" Scott pulled the desk chair so that he could sit facing her. "Were there any background noises that might give us a clue as to where he was?"

"I heard traffic, but almost anywhere in the city you'd expect to hear that. And he sounded good, actually. I don't mean happy, but he sounded stronger. More like the Scott he was before he got sick. He sounded more sure of himself, not as agitated. Which is funny, considering what he was saying to me. I mean, I think he was really afraid, but he wasn't panicking. Does that make sense?"

"I think so, yes. Maybe the time in the hospital did him some good."

"I hope so. I still worry when I don't know where he is."

"You've tried calling him?"

"Yes. But my calls go straight to voice mail." She glanced at the television. "The one thing that gives me hope is that I think he'll stay in town for the race finish on Sunday. He has a lot of friends and former teammates competing and I don't think he'll want to miss it. I'm hoping I'll be able to find him then."

"I'll be looking for him, too," Luke said. "I'll ask the other members of the team to keep an eye out for him, as well."

"Then I'm happy to take advantage of your talent for recognizing faces." On the TV, footage played of crowds gathered at the finish line in Colorado Springs. "I haven't heard anything about any threats or worries about bombings," she said. "Is that because you're asking the press to keep things low-key, or because the danger has lessened?"

"We haven't had any direct threats, but our intelligence tells us the bomber has targeted this race. The Union Cycliste Internationale has asked the press to soften reports of violence, not us. We're working with local law enforcement to make security as tight as we can, though it's difficult when the crowds are stretched out for miles. The UCI won't allow barriers or fences."

"It's against tradition. Cycling is a very fan-oriented sport."

"Except one of those fans might be out to kill people."

"We don't like to believe we live in a world like that." She switched off the TV and stretched her arms over her head. "I think I need to get out of this hotel room for a while. Being cooped up in here all day is making me nuts."

"Let me take you out. We can grab a drink, maybe a bite to eat. I'm betting you skipped lunch."

"How is it that you already know me so well?"

Her smile made him a little light-headed. He'd known she would be worried about her brother, and he knew just what that worry felt like. "I skipped lunch, too," he said. "And I'd like to spend some time with you that doesn't revolve around work."

"That's the best idea I've heard all week." She stood. "Give me a minute to change."

She retrieved some items from her suitcase and went into the bathroom. Luke stood and walked to the window, which offered a view of downtown streets filled with cars and bicycles. Pedestrians strolled the sidewalks or relaxed in a small park on the corner. The bright banners advertising the cycling challenge added color to the scene. He understood why people found it hard to believe others would want to destroy such peace and beauty. Yet he and his team and the other men and women like him who worked on the front lines knew the danger was all too real.

Every day they were getting closer to the terrorists responsible for the London and Paris bombings, but would they stop them in time—before they caused a tragedy on American soil?

The bathroom door opened and Morgan emerged, young and feminine in a flowered summer dress and silver high heels. "You look beautiful," he said.

"Thank you." She picked up her purse from the desk. "You aren't going to get into trouble with your boss for going out with me, are you?" she asked.

"I have a right to a personal life." Though Blessing might not see things that way. "Should we walk or drive?" he asked.

"Walk. It's a warm night and there are so many good restaurants downtown."

They found a bistro with outdoor seating and ordered craft beers and an appetizer sampler. She sat back in her chair and sighed. "I could live in Colorado," she said. "In Texas it's too hot to sit outside like this in August."

"One of the houses we lived in when I was a kid had a screened-in sleeping porch off the upstairs bedrooms," he said. "Mark and I slept out there all summer long—sometimes right up until the first snow."

"My dad would let Scott and I set up a tent in the backyard sometimes in the summer. We'd play tag in the dark, then sit around in the tent with a flashlight and scare each other with ghost stories." Her smile was wistful. "Whenever I see homeless people with packs and bedrolls, I wonder how many nights Scott has spent camping out because he had to, where there are so many scarier things than ghost stories."

Luke took her hand and squeezed it. "The not knowing is hard, I know."

"You do know, don't you?" She turned her

hand over and twined her fingers with his. "I hope you find your brother, and that he's okay."

"I won't stop looking until I find him," he said. "And I won't stop looking for Scott, either."

The waiter brought their food and they fell into the easy silence of two people who don't have to speak to communicate. "Would you like another drink?" he asked, when her beer mug was empty.

"I think what I'd really like to do is take a walk," she said. "Just to enjoy the evening."

"That sounds like a great idea." He paid the bill and they set out. When he held out his hand, she laced her fingers with his and bumped her shoulder against him, as if they'd known each other for years instead of only a few days.

They joined the pedestrians on 16th Street Mall, maneuvering around a clot of excited teens in matching T-shirts who were all talking at once as they took in the sights, then pausing to listen to a busker playing a guitar on the street corner. Morgan tossed a couple of dollar bills into the open guitar case before they continued down the street.

"We have to check out the Tattered Cover," she said, pointing toward the sign for the venerable Denver bookstore.

They waited for a mall bus that had stopped to unload passengers. Out of habit, Luke studied the faces of the people who stepped off the bus, looking for the familiar features of his suspects. Then the bus doors shut and the vehicle roared away. He focused his gaze once more on Morgan and opened his mouth to ask her what she liked to read. But the screech of tires on pavement and a woman's scream shattered the evening's peace.

He looked up to see a car hurtling toward them. He had an impression of black and chrome, roaring like a malevolent beast. He only had time to shove Morgan out of the way and go diving after her before all hell broke loose.

MORGAN RESISTED THE urge to pinch herself to prove she wasn't dreaming. This time with Luke had been a magical respite from the stress and worry that had wounded her heart for the past few days. How was it that, with all the things she had to be unhappy about, with him she could find such peace and contentment?

She had turned to him, to ask this question, when he shoved her hard. She fell, crying out as her knees struck the pavement, then Luke landed on top of her and they rolled together out of the way of the car that ran up onto the sidewalk. The roar of the engine was unnaturally loud in her ears and exhaust stung her nose. Screams tore from her throat and she clung to Luke, even as he pushed himself off her.

She struggled to a sitting position in time to see the driver's door of the car pop open and a figure in black leap out. Luke lurched to his feet and took off after the man, who was running like a wide receiver who had intercepted a pass, dodging and weaving, even leaping over obstacles as he raced down the sidewalk with Luke in pursuit.

"Are you okay, ma'am?" Two of the teenagers in green shirts that they'd passed earlier helped Morgan to her feet. The shirts, with black lettering and musical notes against the vibrant green, said something about a choral convention.

"I'm okay. Thanks." She let them help her to her feet and stood between them, staring in the direction the fleeing man and Luke had run. She could no longer see them for the press of people around her.

"That guy must have been drunk," someone said.

"I don't know," someone else said. "He looked like he was aiming right at that couple."

"Let me through, please." At the authoritative tone, the crowd parted and Luke returned to Morgan's side. He had his phone to his ear and was talking to someone even as he moved to her side. "Black Toyota Camry, Colorado Plate Kilo, Victor, Sierra, five, five, five. The driver was headed east on foot down Sixteenth. My guess is he had someone waiting to pick him up. Get a team over here to get what we can off the car. I'm going to take Morgan back to her hotel."

He ended the call and stowed the phone, then turned to her. "Are you okay?"

"Just shook up." She hugged her arms over her stomach. "What happened?"

He pulled her closer, his arm a warm, strong support holding her up and steadying her nerves. "I don't know, but we'll find out."

Local police arrived and Luke pulled her toward them. He identified himself. "The driver ran away," he said. "I can give you a description, but he was wearing a ski mask and gloves, so I don't think it will help much."

"The person who called it in said it looked like he deliberately tried to run someone down," the cop said.

Morgan gasped, then covered her mouth with her hand. Luke pulled her closer. "I've got a team on their way over to process the scene," he said. "We think this might be related to a case we're working on."

"What case is that?" the officer asked, but Luke ignored the question.

"If we find anything, we'll let you know," he said. He dug a card from his pocket and handed it to the officer. "Or if you hear or see anything… I'm going to take Ms. Westfield back to her hotel."

He led her away from the car, his arm still securely around her. "Do you want to walk or take a cab?" he asked.

"I…I guess we'd better take a cab," she said. The memory of the car headed toward them made her stomach clench. "I mean, what if the guy comes back and tries again?"

He raised his hand to flag a passing taxi and helped her into the backseat, then gave the name of her hotel.

Neither of them spoke on the drive over, or in the elevator to her room. Her hand shook so badly trying to slide the key card into the lock that he took it from her and let them in. Once the door was safely locked behind them, he gathered her in his arms and kissed her, a fierce, claiming kiss that went a long way toward numbing the knowledge of how close they had both come to death.

For a long time, even after the kiss ended, they stood with their arms around each other, her head pressed to his chest and listening to the steady, reassuring beat of his heart. When she felt calm enough to speak, she looked up at him. "Do you really think the driver of that car was aiming at us?" she asked.

"We can't know for sure, but it looked that way to me."

"But why? Because the killer recognized you as an FBI agent?"

"Maybe. Danny saw me in the hotel kitchen, remember?"

"Do you think Danny was driving the car?" she asked.

"No. This guy was taller. Thinner. Maybe he's another member of the group Danny is a part of."

"Scott said I was in danger," she said. "Maybe this is what he meant."

"Until I can be sure you're safe, I won't leave you alone," he said.

Her eyes met his, and she felt again the tidal pull of attraction. "I'd like it if you stayed," she said.

"I can sleep on the floor."

He started to pull away, but she tugged him back. "I don't want you sleeping on the floor."

She touched her fingertips to his mouth to stop his protest. "I know what you said before, about not compromising the case or anything, but no one has to know. Can't tonight just be for us?"

He looked into her eyes, and she saw the depth of his desire, matching her own. "Yes," he said. "All right."

They kissed again, but with the barely restrained urgency of two lovers who know the kiss is only a prelude to what is to come. She pressed her body more firmly to his, one hand gripping his shirtfront, the other kneading his shoulder. He slid one hand down her spine and caressed her bottom. "I've been dreaming about holding and touching you this way," he murmured.

"No photographers this time, I swear." Her breathlessness belied the teasing note she was striving for.

"I'm not sure I'd even care." He cradled her face in his hands and kissed her again, a thorough, claiming kiss that left them both just on the edge of control. A whole movie crew could have jumped out from behind the curtains and she wasn't sure she'd even notice.

He pulled away slightly, putting some space between them but continuing to cradle her face, one thumb stroking the side of her mouth. "You're sure about this?" he asked.

"I'm sure." She searched his face, trying to read the emotions there. She saw passion, and a concern that touched her even more than his lust. Luke was a man who cared deeply—she'd already seen that in his dedication to his job. Now she felt that same consideration focused on her. "All I want to know," she said, "is that right now, what we're feeling, doesn't have anything to do with your work or my brother. It's just about us. And who we are and how we feel about each other."

"This is about you and me." He brushed her hair back off her forehead. "It's all about the things you've made me feel since I first saw you in that surveillance video, before we even met."

"How I made you feel?" The idea intrigued her. How could you feel anything for a stranger? Someone whose name you didn't even know? "How did you feel about me?"

"It sounds crazy, but I felt a connection." He put his fist over his heart. "As if I'd found something—someone—I didn't even realize I was looking for."

The words would have made a beautiful dialogue in a movie, but nothing about them felt rehearsed to her. Luke was telling her the truth, and it touched her more than any fancy speeches or smooth lines could have. "That is crazy, but I feel it, too." She wrapped her fingers around the fist that covered his heart. "You're someone I can be myself with. I don't have to apologize for my nomadic job or my ill brother or anything else about me. I have never experienced that with anyone else. I always thought of relationships as tightrope acts. How much of myself could I really reveal? What was I going to have to compromise on? What were we going to end up fighting about because I wouldn't give in? I don't feel that way with you."

"I don't want you to change or give up anything," he said. "How could I, when my life is full of its own complications?"

"I admire your dedication to your job," she said. "And I understand your grief over your brother. But right now, I don't want to talk about any of that. I just want to be with you." She undid another button on his shirt. "Preferably naked, and under the covers."

"One more thing we have in common." He grabbed the hem of her dress and tugged it over her head.

After that, they couldn't get out of their clothes fast enough. While he cleared the bed, she went into the bathroom and returned with a condom. "I was prepared to go down to the gift shop and buy a box," he said, accepting the packet from her.

"I'm glad you didn't have an excuse to leave the room," she said. "I'd worry you might not come back."

"Oh, I'd have come back." He pulled her onto the bed beside him.

She laughed, then he smothered the sound with another kiss, his hands and his mouth skillfully stoking her passion to a simmer once more. He explored her body with the intensity of a detective examining a crime scene, as if he feared missing some crucial detail. She was equally determined to take her time and enjoy the sensation of him—the feel of his skin beneath her hands, the soap and musk scent of him, the play of light across his muscular body. She would only ever have one first time with him, and she wanted to fix the moment in her mind, not for comparison to future efforts, but as a foundation on which to build.

But their patience could only extend so far, and before too long, he levered himself over her and looked into her eyes. "Are you ready for me?" he asked.

"More than ready." And she pulled him to her.

Their lovemaking took on more urgency as they moved together, at first with the awkwardness of new partners, then with more assurance, driven by instinct and need rather than by conscious thought. Her climax thundered through her and he followed soon after, leaving her spent and shaken and more content than she could remember being in the months since Scott's disappearance.

Afterward, they lay in bed, his arm around her shoulder, her head cradled on his chest. He yawned and she playfully pinched him. "It's too early to go to sleep," she said.

"I'm hungry again," he said. "Maybe we should order in pizza."

"And after that?" she asked.

He slid down in bed and nipped at her neck. "After that, I'll be ready for dessert."

Laughing, she rolled toward him and sat up to straddle him. An old-fashioned telephone ring startled her. She glanced at the bedside phone, but it was silent.

"That's mine," he said. He sat up and gently pushed her away. "I'd better answer it."

She pulled the covers around her against the air conditioner's chill as, naked, he climbed out of bed, located his jacket on the floor and dug out his phone. "Hello? Yes. Where are you?"

Those suits he wore didn't really do his body justice. How had she failed to notice just how gorgeous he was? That pizza might have to wait…

Lost in a pleasant fantasy, she paid no attention to the phone call, but the look on Luke's face when he ended the call and turned to her was like a bucket of cold water dumped on her head. "I have to go," he said.

"What is it? What's wrong?"

"A development in the case." He found his boxers and pulled them on. "I'm sorry, I can't talk about it." He looked around the room. "You should be okay here tonight. Call hotel security if you see or hear anything suspicious."

His cold tone and his refusal to look at her frightened her. "Luke, what is going on? What's happened?"

"I'll call you as soon as I can." Jacket and tie in hand, he bent down to kiss her cheek and then he was gone, leaving her alone and confused. Was this what life with a federal agent was like? Or had something more than a routine case development driven him away from her?

Chapter Twelve

Luke stood at the edge of the clearing, out of the way of the crime scene techs, who were measuring, photographing and taking samples of everything from footprints to blood to bullet casings. The rush of water in the nearby creek and the thick screen of pines and oaks muffled the hum of traffic from the expressway half a mile away. If not for the presence of the techs and the yellow crime scene tape that marked off the area, this might have been an idyllic spot for a campsite. A tent, almost obscured by cut pine boughs, huddled on the opposite side of the space, and an ash-filled circle of rocks awaited an evening's campfire.

"A woman who lives in a subdivision back there called in to the emergency operator and said she'd heard gunshots." Special Agent in Charge Blessing, who had met Luke at the scene, pointed to the woods behind the tent. "A few minutes later, the operators got a call that a man had run out onto the freeway, dodging cars. Someone else called in that someone was chasing the man. That caller even snapped a couple of photos with a cell phone."

Blessing angled his phone toward Luke, who studied a grainy, much-enlarged close-up of a man wearing a Boston Red Sox ball cap. "It could be Danny," Luke said. "But it's not clear enough for me to be sure."

Frowning, Blessing pocketed the phone. "That's the same answer I got from everyone else on the team."

"Any photos of the guy he was chasing?" Luke asked.

"Nope. But the local cops did a good job. They brought in a dog, who led the investigators back in here. Looks like whoever was camped out here left in a hurry—didn't take much with him." In addition to the tent, the clearing contained two folding camp chairs, a five-gallon water jug and a plastic milk crate that held dishes and cooking utensils.

"Homeless people camp along the creek here, don't they?" Luke asked.

"Yeah, but this is no typical homeless person's camp," Blessing said. "There's too much stuff here, and it's all high-end. That tent retails for upwards of two hundred dollars, they tell me."

"How did we end up being called in?" Luke asked. Locals didn't like to share turf with the feds unless they had a good reason.

"That's where things get really interesting."

Blessing indicated the techs processing the scene. "We're not getting much here right now because the Denver cops already did a thorough job. There was a lot of evidence at the scene." He indicated the orange evidence markers that dotted the clearing. "One of the first things they spotted when they came in was a cell phone on the ground. It was smashed up, but they were able to get a set of prints off it. When they ran them, they came up with a name we'd put out an alert for. The lead investigator was smart enough then to put the brakes on and call us."

A chill swept over Luke in spite of the warm night. "What was the name they came up with?" Though he thought he already knew.

"Scott Westfield." Blessing fixed his gaze on Luke, watching for his reaction. "He was here, probably not too long before those nine-one-one calls came in. From the description the Denver cops got from drivers on the freeway, we think he was the guy who ran out in traffic."

"The one the guy in the Red Sox cap was shooting at?"

"We think so."

"What happened to him? Was he hurt?"

"No. He managed to dodge the cars and disappeared. We've got the phone and we're going to see if we can get any call records, see who he talked to in the last couple of days. That might give us some leads."

Luke blew out a breath and looked around the campsite again. The chairs were lined up precisely beside the tent, which was zipped up tight. Neatly split logs formed a pyramid beside the fire ring. "Were there any signs of a struggle here—other than the smashed phone?"

"A couple of bullet casings, some scuffs in the dirt—that's about it. Whoever was here, they were the meticulous type. We haven't even found any food wrappers or apple cores or other garbage."

"Maybe he took it with him when he left, afraid we'd search it for DNA evidence. Can you tell if one person or two was living here?"

"There's only one sleeping bag in the tent, but maybe our shooter took the other one with him. There are two chairs, and enough supplies for half a dozen people."

A trio of men in bombproof suits filed down the path to the clearing. "What are they doing here?" Luke asked.

"The dog indicated explosives in that foot-locker, so we thought we'd better bring in some experts before we tried to move it." He pointed to the tent and this time Luke noticed the black footlocker in its shadow.

"Come on." Blessing nudged his arm. "We'll leave them to it." He walked away and Luke followed, all the way down the path to the dirt lot where they'd left their cars. Blessing leaned back against his black Camry with the government plates and faced Luke, arms folded across his burly chest, an expression on his face that reminded Luke of the look his father had given him when he confronted him about a detention in school. "I heard you had an interesting night," the commander said.

The Denver police must have shared the information about the incident on the 16th Street Mall. "You heard about the car that tried to run me down," he said.

"I also heard who you were with."

Luke stiffened but said nothing. Blessing was sure to quash any defense he made.

"Your personal life is none of my business," Blessing said. "Except when it might jeopardize a case. What were you doing with Morgan Westfield last night?"

An image of a naked Morgan, beneath him in bed, flashed into his head. The scent of her still clung to him. The memory of her touch was still imprinted on him. But he wasn't about to share that with his boss. "We didn't discuss the case," he said.

"Agent Renfro, I shouldn't have to tell you that you cannot be involved with the sister of a suspect in this case." He held up a hand to cut off Luke's objection. "We don't know Scott Westfield's role in all this, but he's clearly up to his neck in something."

"Danny was chasing him," Luke said. "He may have fired shots at him. That doesn't sound like they were on the same side."

"Maybe they were partners and they got into an argument," Blessing said.

Luke looked at the ground. He couldn't argue with his boss's logic, but he resisted the idea that Morgan was a danger to him or to this case.

"Has Ms. Westfield heard from her brother since he left the hospital?" Blessing asked.

"He called her yesterday afternoon, before

she talked to me. He told her she was in danger and that it wasn't safe for him to see her."

"So she called you and told you this?"

"Yes."

"Anything else?"

"He told her to stick close to her cop friend—to me." The memory of this detail strengthened his confidence in her, and in Scott. He wouldn't have told her to stick close to the cops if he was working against them.

"Did he say that because you'd keep her safe, or because he wanted her to keep an eye on you?" Blessing's gaze was shrewd, assessing.

Luke stifled a sigh of frustration. "I don't know. I didn't hear the conversation. I only know what she told me." And what he believed in his gut.

"We'll have someone watch her to see if she contacts him, but you have to stay away," Blessing said. "If you don't, I'll send you back to Washington so fast you'll get a nosebleed."

Luke squared his shoulders and looked the commander in the eye. "Yes, sir." No matter how much it would hurt to break the news to Morgan, he'd sworn an oath that, if necessary, he would forfeit his life in service to his country. Right now, that meant forfeiting the desires of his heart, as well.

THE FIFTH DAY of the Colorado Cycling Challenge took the riders from the small community of Woodland Park, outside of Colorado Springs, to the popular ski town of Breckenridge. Morgan sat on the end of the bed in her hotel room and watched French rider Gabrielle Martiniere claim the yellow jersey for that day's stage, as crowds of onlookers pressed around him, waving French flags and shouting in a cacophony of languages.

She switched off the television and stared at her laptop screen, where she managed to write a halfhearted summary of that day's action for the blog. The race had been an exciting one, and Martiniere's surge in the last few miles to take the lead had been a surprising develop-ment, the kind of thing that was sure to have race fans talking into the night.

But she felt none of that excitement now, and worried her lack of enthusiasm would come through to her readers. No matter how hard she tried, she couldn't distract her mind from worrying about Scott and Luke.

She hadn't heard anything from Scott since their cryptic conversation yesterday after-noon. Her calls to his phone had gone straight to voice mail. Luke hadn't contacted her or answered her calls, either. Of course, he was busy. When the man you loved was occupied with saving the world you didn't expect him to call you every hour to whisper sweet nothings. But Luke's attitude when he left her last night had been so odd. She could practically see him erecting an emotional wall between them.

She'd scoured the papers and internet for any news that might explain Luke's silence but had come up with nothing. The absence of any news about the search for the bomber struck her as a little creepy. The Union Cycliste Internationale had pointedly refrained from any mention of the terrorist activities that had marred the Paris and London races. From their press kits to television interviews granted by UCI officials, they emphasized that the races were safe and that the United States was taking extraordinary security measures to protect both racers and spectators. Then they quickly changed the subject, preferring to talk about the scenic route, the exciting competition and the integrity of the race rather than the horror that made Morgan more and more uneasy as the race neared its finish.

The press had, for the most part, gone along with the charade of pretending that nothing was out of the ordinary about this race. The cause of Alec Demetrie's death had not been released and authorities had allowed speculation that the UCI president had died of natural causes to flourish. If asked about the bombings or any fear they might have for their safety, the racers brushed off or outright ignored the question. Spectators always expressed optimism; perhaps anyone who was afraid stayed home. And certainly the government wasn't saying anything. Maybe they took the view that the fewer people who knew about their activities, the less the chance that information would get back to the wrong person.

She checked the clock. Almost five. Was it too much to hope that Luke would call and ask her to dinner? Or that they'd be able to spend another night together? She hated this aspect of new relationships. Should she wait for him and risk being seen as dependent or clingy, or assert her independence and maybe come across as cold and indifferent? She wanted to be the serene, mature woman who didn't need a man to complete her, but the truth was, she wanted to be with Luke. She wanted to make love to him, but she also simply enjoyed his company, talking with him, working alongside him, simply being in his presence. That didn't make her weak or dependent. Maybe it only made her in love.

In love. A crazy idea, considering the short time they'd known each other. But how else to explain the closeness she felt to him? She wasn't a person who gave her heart easily, but somehow she'd handed it over to Luke Renfro without question.

She snatched up her phone and scrolled to his number before she could change her mind. This time, he answered on the third ring. "Morgan. I was just going to call you," he said.

Then why didn't you? she thought, but she refrained from voicing the snarky question. "Are you busy with work?" she asked.

"Yeah. Really busy." Silence stretched; she thought she heard traffic noises behind him.

"Where are you?" she asked.

Instead of answering her question, he said, "I'm afraid I've got bad news."

His tone of voice, as if he had to force out every syllable, as much as the words themselves, sent a shock wave through her. She couldn't breathe. "Scott?" she managed to whisper.

"As far as I know, he's fine. This isn't about him. At least, not directly."

"Then what is it? What's going on?" He didn't sound like himself, the confident, in-control agent. "You're scaring me."

"I can't see you anymore. Or at least, not until this investigation is over."

At first, she wasn't sure she'd heard him right. "What do you mean? What's happened?"

"I can't talk about it. I've said too much already. Just—I'm sorry. I've asked the local police to keep an eye on you, just in case. I have to go now. Take care."

He hung up. She stared at her phone, wishing more than anything that the technology was available that would allow her to reach right through the screen and shake him. She hit the redial button, but her call went straight to voice mail. "Coward," she said out loud, though she could think of a dozen less-complimentary names to hurl at him.

She tossed the phone onto the bed and began to pace, replaying the conversation over and over in her head. One of her journalism professors, a long time ago, had told her that the key to analyzing an interview was to look at what wasn't said as well as what was said. Luke hadn't sounded angry or indifferent just now. In fact, he'd spoken like a man who was struggling to keep it together. Not having visual clues didn't help, but she couldn't equate the man she'd come to know with a cad who would toss a woman aside after he'd spent the night in her bed.

No, this had to have something to do with his work. He'd said he couldn't see her until after the investigation. Maybe his boss had learned he'd spent the night with her and threatened to fire him if he didn't give her up. As romantic as it might be to picture a man giving up his job for her, that wasn't a particularly smart or practical thing for a guy to do. And when your job was protecting the country, giving it up for almost any reason might even be seen as a dereliction of duty.

Great. The man she loved was…maybe…putting the safety of his country before his personal feelings? This didn't make her feel any better. Why couldn't she have fallen for a chef or scientist or even a fellow journalist? None of them would be able to get away with canceling a date because they had to save lives instead.

And what about when the investigation was

over? Would this fire between them have cooled to the point where he would have lost interest?

Or what if she was wrong about all of this and he was really just being a jerk? She kicked the desk, making her computer jump and her toe throb. Men! Why did they have to make her life so difficult?

Chapter Thirteen

Scott waited across from the convenience store until the parking lot was empty and he was sure the clerk was alone. The midday sun beat down on the pavement and he could smell the mouthwatering aroma of onions and roasting lamb from the Middle Eastern restaurant next door. He remembered eating shish kebab and flatbread at a similar place with Morgan one of the last times he'd seen her in Austin. He'd teased her about the young waiter, who flirted with her; the memory of her laughter brought a sharp sadness to his chest. Would the two of them ever be so comfortable with each other again?

Sure that the coast was clear, he crossed the street slowly, just a dude strolling over to get a soda and a bag of chips. He kept his head down, shoulders hunched to hide his face, aware of the camera aimed at the door.

Inside the store, a plump older woman with a blue streak in her hennaed hair looked up at him. "Hello," she said, regarding him warily. "Can I help you?"

"Yeah. You sell phones?"

She pointed to a display of pay-as-you-go phones on a rack by the register. He scanned the display, skipping over the more expensive smartphones and settling for one that would allow him to text and call, for fifteen dollars. He laid it on the counter. "I'll take this one."

"You need to buy minutes to activate it," she said.

"Oh, yeah." He knew that. He chose the cheapest air-time card—an hour for twenty dollars. He pulled his wallet from the back pocket of his jeans and checked his cash. This wasn't going to leave him much for food or anything else until he could work again.

The woman scanned the phone and the card. "You know how these work?" she asked, not as if she thought he was an idiot, but because she had that motherly attitude he'd seen in a lot of older women.

"Yeah, I'm good," he said, then added, "Thanks."

"That'll be thirty-seven dollars and fifty-two cents," she said.

He handed over his last two twenties and waited while she made change, his foot bouncing.

"You okay?" she asked. "You look kinda pale."

"Yeah. I'm just in a hurry."

"All right." She studied him. Maybe she was

trying to memorize his face. Or maybe she was remembering seeing his face on the news—if the police had put it out there. He hadn't seen a television since he'd left the hospital, so he didn't know. He grabbed the phone and card and his change and ran out of the building. When he looked back, the clerk had picked up her phone and was holding it to her ear, staring after him.

He made himself walk along the sidewalk until he was out of sight of the store, then he raced into an alley between a dentist's office and a women's resale boutique. With shaking hands, he tore the phone from the package. If the clerk had turned him in to the police, he might not have much time. The plastic that encased the phone sliced the side of his hand, drawing blood. He sucked on the wound, which made him think of vampires. He looked around the shadowed alley. If he was a vampire, this would be the kind of place he'd hang out.

His hands shook so badly he had to try half a dozen times to punch in the right code numbers to activate the phone. The charge showed only 25 percent power, but there wasn't anything he could do about that. It wasn't as if he had anyplace to plug it in out here. Maybe later he could find a library and hang out there for a while.

He slipped the phone card into his pocket, in case he needed the numbers again, and felt the punch card of medication he'd brought with him from the hospital. He couldn't remember when he'd last taken his pills. Without the phone alarm to remind him, he had lost track.

He wished now he'd gotten a Coke or some juice from the convenience store. Swallowing the pills without any liquid was hard, but he made himself do it. Then he took a deep breath and punched in Morgan's number.

One, two, three… By the fifth ring he was

ready to hang up when she answered, sounding out of breath. "Hello?"

"Hey," he said. Then, in case the one word wasn't enough for her to recognize him, he added "It's me. Scott."

"Scott!" The way her voice soared, as if she was so happy to hear from him, made his chest tight. No one else ever greeted him that way; he realized how much he'd missed it. "It's so good to hear from you," she continued. "I've been so worried. Are you okay? Where are you? Can I see you? Do you need anything?" The words rushed out, like air escaping from a punctured balloon. The anxiety in her voice ratcheted up his own nervousness, and he bounced his leg again. He felt as if he had Ping-Pong balls ricocheting off the inside of his chest and stomach.

"I'm okay," he said. "You don't need to worry about me."

"Of course I'm going to worry, as long as

I don't know where you are and what you're doing." Wind noise filled his ear, or maybe she was shifting the phone around. He heard the murmur of voices, as if she was in some public place. "Scott, please be honest with me," she said. "Are you in trouble? If you are, I promise to help you, but you have to level with me."

"I'm not in trouble." At least, he didn't think he was. He hadn't done anything wrong. He'd left the hospital before he was supposed to, but that was because Danny was after him.

"Have you seen Danny?" Morgan asked.

He hesitated. How much should be tell her?

"Scott, have you seen Danny?" she repeated.

"I heard you." He chewed the inside of his mouth, struggling with how much to tell her. But that's why he had called, wasn't it? "We had a fight. I went to his camp to talk to him—to tell him to leave you alone. He tried to shoot me."

"Scott!" Her voice rose, too loud in his ear. He held the phone away. "Don't yell at me."

"I wasn't yelling at you, I just… Are you hurt?"

"No. He missed." He stood up straighter. He felt good about that. He'd been too fast. Too clever. Or maybe Danny was just a lousy shot. "I ran away."

"Where are you calling me from? This isn't your number."

"He smashed my phone. I had to get a new one. Listen, I don't want to talk about my phone." He needed to conserve his minutes. "I called to tell you to be careful. Danny is really bad. I didn't realize how bad. He's got a gun and…and I think he might want to hurt racers. He acts like a fan, but I don't think he really is."

"Scott, do you know anything about the bombs that went off at the races in London and Paris? Was Danny involved in that?"

"I don't know. I just saw him in London—I didn't know him. But I get a bad feeling about him. You have to stay away."

"I promise I won't go anywhere near Danny," she said. "But you need to tell all this to my friend Luke. He's with the FBI and they're trying very hard to catch Danny and stop him from hurting people."

"Is Luke the cop I saw you with?"

"Yes, and he is trying hard to find Danny. You could help."

"I don't see how I could help. I don't know where Danny is. I haven't seen him since he tried to shoot me."

"You can tell Luke everything you know— where you saw Danny last, what he was doing, things like that. It might help save a lot of lives."

"I don't know." He looked around. Despite the meds he'd taken, his anxiety was ramping up. He had to get out of this alley. "I've got to go now." He needed to be alone, so he could think.

"Wait. Let me give you Luke's number. Call him. He can help you."

"I don't have anything to write on."

"Fine. When we hang up, I'm going to text the number to you. Promise me you'll call him."

"Maybe. I don't know. I just want you to be safe. I have to go now."

He ended the call before she could try to talk him into doing something he wasn't sure was right. Before he had gotten sick, people had always said he had good judgment. That he'd been smart. A good person. But no one had said that about him in a long time. It was as if the devils in his head were determined to steal who he really was. He had to fight them, to hang on to himself for as long as he could.

MORGAN STARED AT the phone, dragonflies battling in her stomach. All this time, Luke had been saying that Scott could be the key to stopping a killer; now she knew he'd been right. But she wasn't sure if Scott realized yet how important the information he had could be. He hadn't exactly promised to call Luke himself, and they were running out of time. The race ended tomorrow. In Paris and London, the bomber had attacked at the race's finish line. Scott might be the only one who could help stop a similar tragedy here in Denver.

Morgan would have to put aside her hurt over the way Luke had ended things between them and call him. Maybe he could track down Scott through his new phone number.

Afraid he might ignore a call from her cell phone, she used the phone in her hotel room. "Agent Renfro," he answered, his voice brisk, all business.

"Luke, it's me, Morgan. Please don't hang up. I just heard from Scott. What he told me might be important."

"I wouldn't hang up on you," he said. "You didn't stop being important to me just because I have to keep my distance for a little while."

His words, and the warmth behind them, washed over her like a soothing balm, easing some of the tension in her shoulders. She wanted to tell him how good it was to hear his voice and how much she'd missed him, but they didn't have time for those personal feelings, not with so much else at stake. "Scott said he saw Danny. Yesterday, I think. He went to talk to him, to tell Danny to leave me alone. He said Danny shot at him." Her voice caught on these last words, as the enormity of what her brother had told her hit.

"Neighbors heard the shots and called it in," Luke said. "We didn't find any evidence that Scott was hurt."

He'd known about this and hadn't told her? She pushed aside the feeling of betrayal. She didn't like that Luke's job meant he had to keep some things from her, but she had to learn to accept it. "He said he was okay, physically, at least. But he thinks Danny may be mixed up in the bombing."

"Did he say why he thought that?"

"Danny was asking him a lot of questions about the race and the racers, but Scott said they weren't the kind of questions a real fan would ask. I gave him your number and told him he needs to call you and tell you what he knows."

"He needs to contact me soon," Luke said. "We don't have much time."

"That's why I called," she said. "I have his new phone number."

"We found his smashed phone near where the neighbors reported gunfire. We wondered what he and Danny were doing together."

"Is that why you said you couldn't see me? Because you'd discovered evidence that Scott and this Danny guy knew each other?"

"We didn't know what their connection was," he said.

She wanted to argue that there was no connection, but how did she really know that? The most important thing was for Luke to find Scott and talk to him. Then he'd know for sure her brother was innocent. "Will you call him?" she asked. "Or maybe you can track him somehow, using the cell number."

"We'll try. What's the number?"

She read off the number. "Thanks," Luke said. "I'll do my best to reach him. If you talk to him in the meantime, try to find out where he is and I'll go to him."

"If you find him, will you arrest him?" she asked. "He swore he didn't know Danny before a few days ago, though he had seen him in London."

"He hasn't been charged with any crime," Luke said. "We only want to talk to him and find out what he knows. But if he doesn't come forward voluntarily, it could look bad for him, since we know he and Danny know each other."

"It's hard for me to hear you say things like that," Morgan said.

"I know. But you and I are on the same side, truly," he said. "And I'm glad Scott wasn't hurt and is all right."

"He's not all right. He's out there alone and scared and a terrorist wants to kill him. You have to help him."

"I promise I will. I know this is hard," he said. "Especially with things so unsettled between us. But you need to trust me. I'm good at my job. I'll look after Scott, and I'll look after you, too, even though you may not always see me or know that I'm there."

"I do trust you." In spite of everything—years spent looking after herself, his suspicions about Scott and this new distance between them—

she did trust him. Perhaps from the moment they had met, she'd known Luke was a man she could depend on.

Chapter Fourteen

"Our suspect is going to make his move soon. We need to be prepared." Ted Blessing faced the members of Search Team Seven, his brow furrowed with grim determination. Late-afternoon sun slanted through the windows of the hotel conference room illuminating the drab surroundings. The finish of the Colorado Cycling Challenge bike race was less than twenty-four hours away and Luke doubted any of them would sleep before then.

"Maybe we've scared him off," Jack Prescott said. He sat back at one end of the table, tie loosened, an open can of Red Bull in one hand.

"When he abandoned his camp, he left behind all those explosives. He might not have time to assemble more."

"Two pounds of C-4." Cameron Hsung read from the report they'd all received earlier today. "Blasting caps. Maps of the race course."

"He didn't get all of that by himself," Travis said. "Someone probably picked him up from the hotel the night of the banquet, and we don't think he was driving the car that tried to take out Luke and Morgan. We need to be alert for any accomplices."

"We got a match from IAFIS on fingerprints inside the footlocker." Blessing passed around a sheet with a photo of a clean-cut young man in military fatigues. "His name is Daniel Bradley. Thirty years old, honorably discharged from the United States Army in 2011 after service in Iraq and Afghanistan. No priors. No known association with terrorist groups. Though that doesn't mean he hasn't hooked up with a group we don't know about."

"That's the guy we've been looking for," Travis said. "What's his beef with bicycle races?"

"We don't know," Blessing said. "But poisoning the UCI president and the attack on Agent Renfro and Ms. Westfield shows an escalation of violence."

"We've got enough evidence to put this guy away forever," Cameron said. "Knowing we've got that would make most crooks think twice."

"Maybe," Blessing said. "But it could also make him even more determined to complete his mission."

"He can get more explosives," Luke said. "Maybe not high-grade C-4, but an old-fashioned pipe bomb can still do a lot of damage."

"He may already have all the material he needs." Blessing tossed a computer printout onto the table. "I just heard from our friends at the Denver Police Department. Jefferson

County Sheriff's Office reported the theft of ammonium nitrate and fuel oil pellets— ANFO—from a quarry sometime early this morning. The thief disabled the security camera, cut off the lock and was in and out before the night watchman at the place had finished his rounds."

"Could be our guy," Travis said. "Or it could be some other nut."

"What I want to know is why can't we catch this guy?" Luke asked. "We've got all the resources of the United States government behind us, and every law enforcement agency in the state is looking for him. And he's making us all look like a bunch of idiots."

"What about his friends who had the house in Five Points?" Jack asked. "Maybe he's hiding out with them."

"Every indication is they left the city," Blessing said. "We have one lead that suggests they may be operating on the western slope. Possibly near Durango. We haven't been able to pinpoint anything solid but we're still looking. Right now we're focusing our resources on the race. Agent Mathers, give us the rundown on the schedule for tomorrow."

Gus stood and directed their attention to the screen behind him, which showed a map of the downtown area. "The racers will leave Boulder about twelve thirty," he said. "They'll travel toward Golden via Highway 93." He traced the route, from Golden, over Lookout Mountain and into Denver. "After three laps of the downtown area, they'll come up the 16th Street Mall to Union Station, to the plaza behind the station, over the underground bus transit center. The first racers should start arriving between three thirty and three forty-five. The winner's podium and press area are here." He indicated an area of the plaza, between the historic Union Station building and the orange neon sign that proclaimed Travel by Train and the new transportation hall, with its swooping white canopy and glass walls. "There will be grandstands set up on the plaza here." He indicated an area next to the commuter rail tracks. "This entire area will be barricaded. The only way in or out is through a metal detector."

"Except if you're a rider," Luke pointed out.

Gus's pointer stilled. "Yes, except if you're a rider."

"Do you think he'd try to pass himself off as one of the racers?" Travis asked.

"How would that work, unless it's a suicide bomb?" Cameron asked.

"We can't rule out the possibility of a suicide bomb," Blessing said. "But can our man pass himself off as a racer?"

"All the top riders—the ones expected to arrive at the finish line first—are pretty well-known," Travis said.

"But he could wait until later in the race, when the less-well-known racers started to arrive," Luke said. "There would still be plenty of people in the grandstands and press and other racers milling about."

"We can't frisk every rider who comes into that plaza," Jack said. "The UCI would have a cow. And the press would have a field day, too."

"We stop them before they get to the press, before they get into downtown, and search them then," Blessing said.

"It won't keep someone from sneaking into the race after the checkpoint," Travis said.

"We're going to blanket the course with security," Blessing said. "No one is going to get in or out."

"The UCI won't like it," Jack said.

"They won't," Blessing agreed. "But I think the specter of a third bombing, which could very well destroy their sport, will persuade them." He turned back to the map. "Each of you will be stationed somewhere in this area, tasked with searching for Danny and any of the others on our suspect list. This guy and his friends aren't going to get anywhere near the race course." He turned back. "Try to get some rest tonight. We're going to be on the job early, at 6:00 a.m. I'll keep you apprised of any new developments between now and then."

Luke and Travis left the room together. "Do you really think any of us will sleep tonight?" Luke asked.

"I'm going to try," Travis said. "Need to be alert for tomorrow. You?"

"I'm going to keep trying to reach Scott Westfield. I can't help thinking he knows where Danny is—even if he doesn't realize it."

"He won't answer your calls, huh?"

"No, and he hasn't been in touch with Morgan again, either."

"Have you seen her?"

"No." But they'd stayed in touch. He'd kept the conversation focused on Scott and his job.

He was sticking to the letter of his agreement with Blessing. He didn't know where the case would end up, but he wanted to leave the door open for Morgan. She was too special for him to lose without a fight. "She promised to let me know if she heard from Scott. I tried to put a trace on the phone, but didn't have any luck. We just don't have enough time left."

"It's making me crazy that this guy keeps giving us the slip," Travis said. "It's like he can turn himself invisible or something. I mean, the whole point of this team is to see people, the way other people don't see them. But we're not stopping him."

"I drove around the area near the camp for over an hour last night, hoping to see Danny or Scott." Luke shook his head. "No luck."

"Gus says the key is to go all Zen and think like these guys do, but that doesn't seem to be helping him any."

"I'd try anything if I thought it would work," Luke said.

"Pray that we catch a break tonight or tomorrow," Travis said. "I have a feeling that's the only way we're going to stop this guy."

They parted at the street, Travis headed for his car, Luke to walk downtown. While he scanned the faces of those around him, he tried to puzzle out where Scott might be. He'd left the camp on foot, running. He was concerned for his sister and wanted to stay close to her. To watch over her, even. And he felt a connection to the racers and the bike race. So maybe he would stay close to the course, also. The people Luke had interviewed at the men's shelter where Scott had been living seemed to think he and Danny had met at the shelter. And Scott may have been sharing Danny's camp down by the creek. So he wasn't a loner. He sought out the company of others on the street.

He set out walking in the direction of Union

Station, but instead of heading toward the up-scale restaurants and high-rise apartments that flanked the transportation hub, he detoured to a soup kitchen he'd seen advertised on a church sign. Half a dozen men lounged on the steps of the church in the sun. A sign advertised the kitchen would open in another hour.

A definite chill set in when he approached the group. Even if he hadn't been dressed in his suit, he knew everything about him screamed "cop" to these streetwise men. "I'm looking for a friend of mine," he said. He scrolled to his photo of Scott and held it toward them. "His name is Scott. Have any of you seen him around?"

"What you want him for?" A burly black man with a beard fixed a hard stare on Luke.

"He hasn't done anything wrong," Luke said. "His sister is worried about him and she asked me to look for him. I only want to talk to him and make sure he's okay."

The only answer he received was stony stares and silence. If he told these men that the lives of dozens, even hundreds, of people might depend on him finding Scott, would they believe him? Would they even care?

"I seen him yesterday, down by the tracks." A younger man, thin with a pockmarked face, spoke up.

"The tracks? The train tracks?"

"Light rail. Perry Station. He was sitting under a tree. Might be he stays around there."

Luke thanked the man and took off at a trot for the light rail station on Eighteenth. He scanned the route map and hopped on the next W train to arrive. Ten minutes later, he got off at Perry Station. New apartments fronted a green space beside the station, next to a neighborhood of older homes in various stages of renovation. A bike path next to the creek led past a playground and basketball courts.

Luke set off along the path, searching for any

place a man might camp for the night, out of sight of cops and nosy neighbors but still close to the trains, which would make it easy to get around the city. After ten minutes of walking, he found what he was looking for—a dirt path that led into the woods behind a gutted factory. A sign beside the factory announced it was being transformed into lofts.

He followed the trail through the woods, noting the empty whiskey bottles, beer cans and fast-food wrappers that littered the underbrush. Before long, he came to a dirt clearing, where an old sofa and a trio of folding chairs were arranged around half a metal barrel. Two men occupied the folding chairs. Scott lay on the sofa, eyes closed.

The men were already standing and moving away when Luke approached. "I'm not here to bother you," he said, and walked over to Scott. He shook the young man gently. "Scott, wake up. It's me, Luke. We need to talk."

THE SIXTH DAY of the race consisted of time trials in the mountain town of Vail. American Andy Sprague claimed the yellow jersey for this stage, and was a favorite to win the race tomorrow, as well. Morgan, sick to death of her hotel room, watched the race results from a tavern on Seventh, surrounded by noisy race fans who cheered on their favorites. She wondered what Scott would think of today's results. In time trials, each racer competed against the clock. They couldn't draft off team members or trade off positions with someone on their team, to allow each other to rest. Scott had always preferred the camaraderie and strategy involved in team racing, but some racers saw time trials as the true test of a racer's ability, so every big race these days incorporated both approaches in the various stages.

The bartender switched the television to a baseball game and Morgan paid for her drink and left the bar. It was too early to return to her room, which had begun to feel more like a prison. She decided instead to walk down toward Union Station, and the finish line. Maybe she'd find inspiration there for the article she had yet to write, summarizing today's race results. And she could scope out the best location from which to watch the finish tomorrow.

The area around Union Station was undergoing a transformation, with work crews hanging colorful banners from every lamppost down the street leading to the finish line. Flags from every country participating in the race snapped in the breeze around the broad plaza, where more workers were assembling a podium and grandstand. Someone had even hung a banner over part of the station's iconic orange neon sign, so that the legend would read Travel by Bike.

She crossed the street at Fourteenth and started toward the grandstands, but she hadn't gone far before a blue-uniformed police officer stopped her. "Excuse me, ma'am, but this area is closed to the public."

"Oh, I'm sorry." She stepped back. Behind him, she could see crews setting up shining metal barriers.

"You can go through the bus station." He pointed up the block. "Go in the doors of the transportation hall, and downstairs. There's an elevator at the end that will take you up to street level on the other side of the plaza."

She glanced at the barriers. "I guess this is all part of security for the race tomorrow."

"Yes, ma'am. We want everyone to enjoy the race safely."

"Thank you." She retraced her steps down the street. This time, she noticed the extra police on duty, and signs notifying race-goers that they must pass through security before taking their place along the final route or entering the plaza. Luke was out here right now, doing his part to keep people safe, too. If only she could contribute more to the efforts.

She rode the escalator down to the bus station beneath transportation hall. The area was packed with people waiting for or disembarking from city buses. She wove her way through the crowd and had almost reached the exit on the opposite side when someone jostled her.

"Excuse me," she said, and tried to move away, but a strong hand grabbed her arm.

"Don't scream," a voice whispered in her ear, and something sharp jabbed at her side.

"What? Who are you?" Fighting panic, she tried to turn her head, to see her attacker, but the knife jabbed, and a sharp pain went through her.

"Walk," the voice commanded, and pushed her forward.

She walked, the man's arm wrapped around her, holding her close, like two lovers making their way through the crowd. Except that one hand gripped the back of her neck to keep her from turning her head or looking at him, and the other held what she guessed was a knife to her side.

He led her, not outside, but to a door marked Custodial. He pulled this open, shoved her inside and then everything went black.

Chapter Fifteen

Morgan's head throbbed. What had she done to end up with such a headache? Was she coming down with the flu or something? And why was this bed so uncomfortable? She opened her eyes and stared at gray concrete. She tried to move her arms and couldn't, then realized she wasn't lying on a bed at all, but on a hard floor. She rolled over again and kicked her feet, trying to get free. She had a dim memory of walking through the transportation hall, of someone grabbing her and then...nothing.

"I wouldn't thrash around so much if I were

you. You don't want to blow us up. At least not yet."

She whipped her head around and saw a man standing in front of a door. He was dressed all in black—black boots, black pants, black long-sleeved T-shirt and a black ski mask over his face. At the mention of blowing up, she gasped. "Who are you? What are you talking about?"

He knelt beside her and adjusted something on her chest. Some kind of vest. It wasn't too tight, but it was definitely heavy. "There are five pounds of pelleted explosives in this vest, as well as several sticks of dynamite," he said. "It's wired to go off at a signal from me, but you should probably lie still, just in case your movement happens to trigger a stray spark. It would be a shame to waste all my efforts before the big day."

He spoke calmly, with an unaccented but definitely American voice. His hands, the only part of him she could see, were white.

"What are you talking about?" she asked. "You sound crazy."

"Your brother is the crazy one. It's a shame, really, I watched some footage of him, racing. He was good. Though probably as corrupt as all of them."

His mention of her brother made her break out in a cold sweat. This had to be Danny. The man who had killed the UCI president. The man who had shot at Scott. The person Luke suspected of being responsible for the bombings in London and Paris. She had to learn as much as she could about him. "Were you a racer, too?" He didn't really have the build for it—he was too soft. "Or was someone you loved a racer?"

"No."

"Then what do you have against racing?"

She felt his gaze on her, though she could see little of him in the ski mask. "Racing represents everything corrupt about this country," he said after a moment.

"I don't understand what you mean."

"I don't require you to understand."

What an odd choice of words. What did he "require" from her? "What are you going to do with me?" she asked. She wasn't sure she really wanted to know the answer to that question, but if she had any chance of surviving at all, she needed to know what was going on in his head.

"The problem with people today is they don't listen." He tightened a strap on the vest and stood once more. "I told you, this is a suicide vest. It's wired to explode at a signal from me. It will kill you, and everyone around you."

"What did I ever do to you that you'd want me to die?" she asked, hating the way her voice shook on the last words.

"You didn't do anything in particular," he said. "But as my mentors have taught me, the best way to get back at the people you hate is to target their loved ones. Your brother and your cop friends are making my life very difficult right now. They're interfering with plans they have no business trying to stop. They must pay for their mistakes, so I'm going to destroy what they love most. You."

Did he really think Luke loved her that way—that he'd be destroyed by her death? She closed her eyes and swallowed back tears. Maybe he did feel that way about her. She knew for sure that she cared for him enough to not want to see him hurt this way. And Scott—to have her death associated with the bicycle racing he still loved could be enough to send him into a madness from which he might never recover.

She opened her eyes and tried as best she could to hide her emotions from his scrutiny even though, as Luke had pointed out, she was a lousy liar. "What are you going to do?"

He took something from his pocket—a purple

cell phone she recognized as her own. "First, I'm going to take a picture." He held up the phone. "Smile."

She stared at him, rigid with fear. The digital shutter clicked and he studied the results on the screen. "That will do," he said. "You look suitably horrified."

"Why do you need a picture?" she asked.

He pocketed the phone. "I'm going to send this to the media, so they'll see what I have planned. But they won't know where or when."

Clearly, he was nuts. She had to get away from him, any way she could. "Fine. You have your picture. You can take the vest off now."

"No." He moved to her side and pulled a bandanna from his pocket. He stuffed it in her mouth as she fought against him. "Remember what I told you about the explosives," he said as he taped the gag in place. "You don't want to set them off too early." He moved to the door and flicked the switch to shut off the light, plunging the room into darkness. "I'll be back in a little while to move you into place," he said.

What then? she wondered.

He anticipated her unvoiced question. "Then, I'll blow you up." The last thing she heard was a choked sound, as if he was chuckling to himself while he shut the door behind him, leaving her alone in the dark.

"I WAS GONNA call you," Scott said. He sat on a bench next to Luke, under a streetlight in a park not far from the sofa where Luke had found him. Ace and Dinky, the guys he'd been hanging with, had left. They didn't want to hassle with a cop. Scott didn't want the hassle, either, but he figured he had no choice. When Luke suggested they walk over here to the park, Scott had followed. He was tired of running, anyway. "I just had to think how to do it," he said. "I don't want to get into trouble."

"You're not in trouble," Luke said. "But I really need your help. I need to know everything you can tell me about Danny."

"Where's Morgan? Is she okay?" Scott had been counting on Luke to look after his sister when he couldn't. If Luke was here with him, that meant Morgan was alone.

"She's fine. I talked to her yesterday."

"Why aren't you with her?" he asked. "I thought you'd look after her."

Luke shifted on the bench. He looked… guilty. "I've been busy," he said. "With work."

"I thought with a cop protecting her, she'd be all right. She could be in danger." Scott fought down his rising agitation.

"I asked the local cops to keep an eye on her."

"That's not the same as having someone looking out for her who really cares."

Luke's face reddened. "Morgan will be okay," he said. "But we have to stop Danny. Do you know where he is?"

Scott shook his head. "I saw him this morning, in the bus station. He didn't know I was watching, but then the crowd cleared out and I was afraid he'd see me. But he left before I did. He got on a bus and I didn't see him any more after that."

"Do you know which bus?" Luke had pulled his phone out of his pocket and was typing something into it.

"No. I didn't see. I got out of there fast. I didn't want him to see me."

"What time was this? I can have someone check the bus schedules."

"Maybe two o'clock? It was after lunch, and before I ran into Ace and Dinky and came here."

Luke nodded. "What else do you know about Danny? Do you know his full name?"

"He never said. And I didn't ask. I mean, it wasn't like he was a good friend or anything. We just…hung out, you know."

"Did you stay at his camp by the creek?"

Scott looked away. The camp was supposed to be a secret.

"We know the two of you argued there. He smashed your phone and he shot at you. Neighbors reported the shots and drivers on the freeway saw you running away."

"I told him he had to leave Morgan alone and he didn't like that."

"What can you tell us about the camp? What kind of things did he have there?"

"Just, you know, camping stuff. But good stuff. New."

"What kind of things?" Luke asked.

"Just…a tent and a sleeping bag and some blankets. A couple of chairs and dishes and food and water. And he had a footlocker, where I guess he kept his clothes and stuff. Or maybe he had money in there. He kept it locked and he didn't like me going near it. Once I made the mistake of sitting on it and he almost bit my head off."

"Did you ever see him open the trunk?"

Scott shook his head. "Not while I was there, but I only stayed there a couple nights, after we left the men's shelter."

"Why did you leave the men's shelter with Danny?"

"Well, you know…he asked me to." He began jiggling his right foot. "I was staying there a couple days and then one day Danny walks in. I sort of recognized him, but couldn't remember him—not really. I thought he was just another homeless dude I'd seen around. But then he comes over and starts talking. He reminds me we saw each other at the bike race in London. He was a fan and he wanted to talk racing, which was cool, you know? Not many people care about racing. But they got mad at us for talking about it. Some of the guys complained and the people who ran the shelter said we had to either shut up or leave. So Danny said we should leave, that he had a nice place down by the creek."

"If he had the place by the creek, why did he come to the shelter at all?" Luke asked.

"I wondered that, too," Scott said. "But he said he came to take a shower, and to ask about day labor jobs. He thought maybe the shelter folks could help him out."

"Okay, so you went to his camp," Luke said. "Did anyone else come with you?"

"No. He didn't ask anyone else."

"Why not?"

"I don't know. Maybe because a lot of those guys are older than us. And Danny said he wanted to talk about racing. They didn't care about that."

"So you talked about racing."

"Yeah. He asked a lot of questions at first. He remembered that I had been a racer and he wanted to know what that was like. He knew a lot of the top racers' names and he asked about them."

"Like a fan would," Luke said.

"At first, yeah. You know, things like 'Is Victor as intense as he seems when he's racing?' and 'Is Andy a good teammate?' But later, he asked other questions. Things that didn't sound so odd to me at the time, but later, when I thought about them, they didn't seem like the kind of things fans would want to know."

"What kinds of things?"

"He wanted to know about the end of the race. How long would it take the top riders to get from Boulder to the finish in downtown Denver? How many of them would arrive at once? How close would the fans be able to get to the winners? How many people would be there? Would the crowds be bigger at the beginning of the finish or did most people stay around to see the end? He wanted to know what kind of security they had at races, what the racers did after they finished—did they leave right away or did they stay to mingle with fans? Some of the questions I didn't know the answer to, but if I couldn't answer them, he'd get angry."

"What did you do then?" Luke asked.

"I started to make up things. And sometimes I lied, just because he annoyed me. He made me feel like he didn't care about me, he was just pumping me for information."

"What did you tell him?"

"I told him all the racers stayed until the end, and the crowd stayed, too, so by the end it was this big, wild party. I told him if he wanted his picture taken with the winners, all he had to do was ask. That's sort of true at some races, though usually you have to be a pretty woman for them to say yes. I didn't tell him that."

"Were you staying at the camp with Danny the day you broke down in the hotel kitchen and were taken to the hospital?" Luke asked.

"I don't know where I would have stayed that night if I hadn't ended up in the hospital," Scott said. "When I told Danny that morning that I was going to work, he got mad. He said I didn't need to go back there. I told him it was a good job and I liked it and the people were nice. I wanted to see Morgan again, too. Danny got really upset. He told me my sister didn't care about me and none of the people at the hotel cared about me—but that he and I were a team. We needed to stick together."

"What did you say to that?"

"Nothing. I just grabbed my stuff and told him I was going to work. He yelled at me not to tell anyone about him. I told him I wouldn't, but I could tell he didn't believe me. So I'd already decided not to go back."

"Except you did go back," Luke reminded him.

"Well, yeah. But only because I was worried

he would hurt Morgan. I needed to tell him to leave her alone."

"He had threatened Morgan?"

"In the hospital." Scott's stomach hurt, remembering the menace in Danny's voice. "He said if I didn't keep quiet he would hurt my sister. And I could tell he really meant it. You get a feeling about people sometimes, you know?"

Luke nodded. "Yeah, I know." He looked at his phone. "I'm going to call in a report that Danny was seen in the bus station this morning. That's very near where the closing ceremonies for the race are going to be held tomorrow."

"Do you think Danny is the one who planted those bombs in London and Paris?" Scott asked. "Do you think he'll try the same thing here?"

Luke hesitated. Scott thought he was deciding whether or not to trust him with the information. "He was in London," Scott said. "And he's been acting so strange here. I heard the

UCI president died—that he was poisoned. I saw Danny doing something with the entrées that night. He'd lifted the lid on one and he really didn't have any business being around the food. When he saw me watching him, he moved away, but he also told me he'd hurt me if I told anyone I saw him. If Danny is the one who poisoned President Demetrie, then he must hate racing."

"We think he could be the bomber," Luke said. "Your coming forward may help us stop him before he kills more people. Thank you. It took a lot of guts to do this."

Scott looked away, trying to control his emotions. "I hate that I can't race anymore, but I still love the sport. Someone trying to hurt the sport—and hurting innocent people that way... It's a lot sicker than I'll ever be."

"You're right." Luke turned to his phone, which sounded a trio of descending notes. "It's a text—from Morgan."

He thumbed the text icon. Scott wasn't looking at the phone, but at Luke, and the FBI agent's face blanched as white as his shirt.

Scott sat up straight. "What's wrong? Are you okay?" Luke looked like he was about to pass out or have a seizure or something. Did Scott remember the CPR he'd learned the summer he was a lifeguard in high school?

"It's Morgan." The words came out choked. Luke turned the phone toward Scott, who stared at the image of his sister. She was tied up and lying on a dirty concrete floor, her eyes wide with terror.

"What's that on her chest?" Scott asked, pointing toward what looked like a radio or a bundle of old highway flares.

"It's a bomb." Luke stared at the picture, some of the color returned to his face now. "The message says, 'I've got a friend of yours. She's going to celebrate the end of the race with a real bang.'"

Chapter Sixteen

Morgan didn't know how long she lay on the floor in that bus station storage room. With her arms bound behind her back and the vest a heavy weight on her chest, she could find no comfortable position. At first, she could see nothing in the dark room, but as her eyes adjusted, she could make out a thin band of light at the bottom of the door. The muffled, hurrying footsteps of people passing through the transportation hall ebbed and flowed with the arrival and departure of the buses, along with scraps of words she couldn't assemble into any coherent conversations. "So he said…

The report… Anthony, wait up!…Nowhere… Did you see?"

After a while, she closed her eyes and turned her attention to trying to get out of the ties that bound her wrists. The plastic or wire or what-ever Danny had used cut into her flesh, draw-ing blood when she struggled too much. She inched on her back toward the door. Maybe she could pound on it with her feet and some-one would hear her. But the first hard kick at the metal sent such a shock wave through her that she gasped, sure she had set off the bomb. After that, she was too afraid to try again. She'd have to wait until Danny returned and try to get away from him then.

If he did return. The thought that Danny might not made her choke on the gag, and she had to force herself to calm down. But maybe he had left her here for good. He would set off the bomb when he was ready. The bus station was right under the transportation hall, next to the plaza. If the explosives were powerful enough, he could do a lot of damage by detonating the bomb here.

But no. He had said he would return. Hadn't he? She was so terrified she couldn't be certain what was real and what was fearful imagining.

Long after the bus station fell silent, the door opened. She startled, not having heard his footsteps. She saw the baggy gray uniform pants first, and a powerful hope made her try to sit up and to cry out from behind the gag. One of the janitors had found her. She was saved.

But then Danny looked down on her, much of his face hidden by oversize sunglasses and a knit cap pulled down low over his forehead. "It's time," he said, and hauled her to her feet.

He pulled her roughly toward a large garbage cart by the door, then, without warning, he picked her up and stuffed her into it. She tried to fight him, but the bindings around her ankles and wrists, as well as his viselike grip, kept her immobilized. He shoved her down into the trash cart, her knees to her chest, then dumped a trash can full of loose papers over her. "One peep from you and you're dead," he ordered, and switched off the light.

He rolled the cart out of the janitor's closet. The tinny strains of classical music and the echoing footsteps of passing people told her they were in the bus terminal. One of the wheels of the garbage cart gave off a high-pitched squeak. Through the screen of papers, she could see the arching canopy of the terminal.

The cart stopped and a fresh load of trash rained down on her—paper coffee cups and food wrappers, old newspapers and soda cans. She ducked her head and closed her eyes against the worst of the onslaught. They continued on, stopping two more times while her captor emptied trash onto her.

Finally, the cart reversed direction. She could

no longer see out of the top of the cart, but she listened for any clues about where he might be taking her. After a few minutes, they stopped, and she heard the familiar *ding* of elevator doors opening.

Inside the elevator, Danny leaned over and pushed the trash aside. He grabbed her by the arms and hauled her out of the can and propped her against the metal handrail that encircled the car. The elevator car was glass on all four sides, with chrome supports. Though enclosed on this lower level, at the plaza level it was a striking glass-and-chrome rectangle that provided handicapped access to the facilities below.

But her captor didn't order the elevator to ascend. Instead, he produced handcuffs from his pockets—two pairs. He untied Morgan's wrists and attached one set of handcuffs to each one. Then he attached the other ends of the handcuffs to the railings on adjacent sides of the elevator. She was trapped in the corner of the elevator, facing the door.

"This elevator is now officially out of order," he said. "This afternoon, when the time is right, I'll send a signal via the building's computer controls to activate the elevator and tell it to ascend. The glass here will give everyone a very good look at you, but before they can do anything, I'll make the call to detonate the bomb and you'll go boom."

Why are you doing this? Silenced by the gag, she tried to telegraph the question with her eyes.

"We live in a corrupt world and violence is the only way to force change," he said. He checked the cuffs to make sure they were securely fastened. "Don't waste your time struggling. You can't save yourself now." He replaced the gag in her mouth and tore off a fresh strip of duct tape. "And neither can your brother or Agent Renfro."

LUKE AND SCOTT arranged to meet the rest of the team in Union Station's security offices, deep in the bowels of the historic train terminal. Antique clocks lined the hallway leading to this sanctum, each showing the time in a different part of the country or the world. But the only clock Luke cared about was the one ticking until the race ended later today, and what could be the end of Morgan's life.

Outside the door to the security office, he stopped and turned to Scott. "Don't say anything unless someone asks you a question," he said. "Some people aren't going to like that I'm involving a civilian at all. You may be asked to leave for part of the meeting, but don't go far. We need your help on this."

Scott nodded. He looked calmer than Luke felt, something he hadn't expected. Maybe he was numb to what was really going on. Or maybe he had it together a lot more than people gave him credit for.

Inside, he found the others crowded into a small conference room to the left of the door. The others scarcely glanced up when Luke and Scott slipped inside. They were too focused on the image of Morgan that Luke had emailed to Blessing, who had it projected onto a screen on the back wall. "Do we know it's a real photo, not a fake?" Jack asked.

"That bomb looks real enough to me," Travis said. "And that's definitely Morgan."

Behind Luke, Scott made a strangled sound in his throat but kept quiet.

"The big question is, how is he going to sneak a woman wired with a bomb onto the scene?" Cameron asked.

"Put her in a muumuu, a raincoat, a minivan. There are probably a hundred ways," Blessing said.

"He'll never get her past a metal detector, with all that hardware," Jack said.

"He'll use a disguise," Luke said. "He's done

it before. First, he was a dishwasher in the hotel kitchen. Then he was an orderly at the hospital. He knows how to blend in."

"So what disguise?" Blessing asked.

"Someone who doesn't have to go through the metal detectors. A cop," Travis said.

"A security guard." Cameron nodded toward the guards in the next room. "There must be a dozen of these guys all over this building," he said. "It would be easy enough for a skilled operative to knock one out and change clothes with him."

The image on the screen switched to a blueprint of the plaza area. "Mr. Westfield."

Blessing's deep, commanding voice made Scott jump. "Y-yes, sir?"

"You know Danny better than any of us. Where do you think he would put his bomb?"

"I don't know him that well," Scott said. "I just met him."

"I'll amend my statement then. You have

spent more time with him than the rest of us, and you've spoken to him more. I want to know your thoughts."

Scott studied the map of the plaza, his brow furrowed. "He wants to go after the bikers. He has a grudge against the racers. And…I think he wants attention. He asked a lot of questions about when the most people and the most press would be around the finish line."

"That fits with his previous pattern," Blessing said. "And bringing an innocent person into his plan fits with the psychologist's prediction of escalating violence."

Luke stared at the plaza map. "We're missing something," he said. "Some flaw in our security that he's going to take advantage of."

"We need to get to Morgan before he brings her to the finish line," Travis said.

"The picture he sent doesn't give us any clues where he's holding her," Cameron said.

"What if he sent the picture to distract us,"

Gus said. "He wants us to focus our resources on rescuing her, while he sneaks in behind us and wreaks havoc."

"Or what if he has two bombs?" Jack said. "One for Morgan and one for the race?"

"I forwarded this image to our explosives experts at Quantico," Blessing said. "They're going to look at close-ups of the bomb and see if that will tell us anything."

"We know he was in the bus station this morning," Luke said. "Do the surveillance videos show anything?"

"I'm already on it." Wade spoke up from the other end of the conference table. "I downloaded the video for the last twenty-four hours. We were able to pick him up leaving about 2:00 p.m., but we can't spot when he came in. He may have come in on one of the buses that arrived before then. It would be pretty easy to get lost in the crowds."

"And you're sure he hasn't been back?" Blessing asked.

"He hasn't shown up on film," Wade said. "And he'd be easy to spot this time of night. The last bus departed at 9:00 p.m. The station is closed until tomorrow at 6:00 p.m. for the bike race. The only people in the hall now are a security guard, and the janitor who went through about an hour ago."

"You're sure of the identity of the guards and the janitor?" Blessing asked.

"I'm one step ahead of you," Gus said. "I already checked with the head of security. He identified every employee we saw on the screen. And I'd have recognized our guy if he was one of them."

Blessing's phone beeped. He answered the call, listened a moment then disconnected. "That was the explosives tech at Quantico," he said. "He thinks the bomb Morgan is wearing in the photo would be remotely detonated.

The most common way to do that these days is with a cell phone. And he reminded me they think the London bomb was remotely detonated, as well."

"Can we block the signal?" Luke asked.

"Yes," Blessing said. "At our first security meeting with the UCI, we suggested it. They objected. People don't like being disconnected—whether we're talking the racers, the fans or the press. We backed down, but now I'm going to ask for a cell phone signal block within a two-mile radius of this station."

"You're betting on the bomber not having an alternate way to set things off," Luke said.

"The explosives tech says the alternatives would require Morgan to manually trigger the bomb, or the bomber would have to get close enough to do it himself." Blessing clapped him on the shoulder. "We're doing everything we can to find her and to stop him."

Luke nodded. "I want to take a look at the

bus terminal again," he said. "See if I spot anything." The terminal was the last place they definitely knew Danny had been. If they only had some way to retrace the bomber's steps.

"All right," Blessing said. "Let us know if you spot anything."

Luke turned to leave. Scott joined him at the door. "Can I come with you?" he asked.

Luke had thought he wanted to be alone, to worry and brood over the case. But Scott's offer gave him a way to avoid what would probably be a pointless exercise. "Yeah. You can show me where you saw Danny last."

They headed outside and crossed the plaza, which was lit up like midday by the portable light towers surrounding it. Half a dozen uniformed officers guarded the space, and the streets leading to the station were already blocked off. Bus and light rail service to the area had been halted until after the race.

"I don't see how anyone could get past all those guards," Scott said.

"We've got spotters in the hotel watching the plaza, as well," Luke said, nodding toward the high-rise hotel that flanked one side of the plaza. "But this Danny guy seems to have a knack for slipping past every trap we set."

The escalators leading down into the bus terminal were shut off. Luke flashed his ID to the guard at the top of the stationary steps, then led the way down into the cavernous space. Their footsteps echoed on the concrete, against a background of piped-in classical music. "You think they would at least shut off the music," Scott said.

"People don't like silence," Luke said.

"It's because they don't like to hear what's in their own heads." He gave Luke a half grin. "You don't have to be schizo to know that."

Luke nodded. The more time he spent around

Scott, the more he liked him. He'd been dealt a bad hand but was doing his best to cope.

They walked the length of the terminal, surveying the empty bus bays and benches. Posters advertised an upcoming musical or advised of bus route changes. Midway down the hall, the handicap elevator bore an out-of-service sign; like the escalators, it was shut down in anticipation of events that afternoon.

Across from the elevator was a door marked Custodial. Luke tried the knob and it opened to reveal a closet that contained a large trash can on wheels, a couple of push brooms and a shelf of toilet paper, soap and other restroom supplies.

"Guess the janitor's already gone home," Scott said.

They exited the other end of the terminal and headed back toward the train station. "There's something we're not seeing," Luke said. He turned to look back at the silent, floodlighted plaza. Flags popped in the night breeze and the podium and grandstand awaited tomorrow's celebration. This was how he'd felt when Mark disappeared. He'd returned to the trailhead again and again, certain that he was missing some important clue that could help him find his brother. But no matter how hard he drove himself, he always came up blank. A man who never forgot a face couldn't remember those two hikers who had been at the trailhead when he dropped Mark off. And now he couldn't spot the clue that would lead him to Danny and to Morgan. What good was a skill like his if he couldn't use it to help the people who mattered most to him?

"Wherever she is, she knows you're looking for her," Scott said.

Luke nodded and turned back toward Union Station. As he and Scott walked back to the security center, the line of clocks taunted him.

Only eleven more hours to find a killer. Only eleven more hours to save the woman he loved.

LUKE SNAGGED A few hours of restless sleep on a cot just off the conference room, but at five he was back in front of the computer, staring at diagrams of Union Station and the plaza, trying to put himself in the mind of a killer.

Scott slid a cup of coffee in front of him, then sagged into a folding chair at his side. "Did you sleep any?" Luke asked.

Scott shook his head. "I don't know whether it's because I'm worried about Morgan or because it's a race day. Even though I'm not racing anymore, I still get that rush of anticipation the night before. I never slept well the night before a race. I raced on nerve and adrenaline. By the time the day was over I was completely wiped. I remember one time I collapsed walking off the winner's podium. My trainer and Morgan hauled me to my feet and sneaked me out by some back elevator so no one would see."

"The race was over. Why did you care if anyone saw?"

"Because when something like that happens, the judges think you must be on something. All I needed was more water, food and rest." He leaned over and pointed to the handicap elevator behind the winner's podium. "That would have been convenient that day. Right by the podium."

The words struck Luke like a hammer blow. He stared at the X within a cube that marked the elevator on the diagram and had an image of the out-of-service sign on the door in the bus terminal. Why would someone bother to put a sign on the elevator when the whole building was closed?

The image in his mind shifted to the janitor's closet across from the elevator. The garbage cart inside the door would be big enough to hold a person.

"Gus!" He whirled in his chair and shouted to the agent across the room.

"What?" Blinking, Gus looked up from his computer.

"Do you still have those security recordings from last night?"

"Sure. What do you need to see?"

"The janitor. Let me see that janitor."

He and Scott hurried to stand behind Gus, who scanned through the videos, fast-forwarding through the arrival and departure of the last few buses of the night. Finally, he slowed and zoomed in on a figure pushing the garbage cart.

The janitor, a stooped man in a baggy jumpsuit with a black stocking cap pulled low, exited the custodian's room with his cart and proceeded through the terminal, pausing now and then to empty a trash can. Finally, he headed back toward his closet. But instead of stowing the trash can there, he crossed the hall and pressed the button to open the elevator. He pulled the cart in after him and the door closed.

Luke swore and pounded his fist against the table. "How could we be so stupid?" he said. "That's Danny. It has to be."

"Come on." Gus pointed to the screen. "This guy is older and fatter. And the security chief here swore it was the regular janitor."

Travis and Blessing joined them in front of the monitor. "What's going on?" Blessing asked.

"I've found Danny." Luke indicated the figure on screen. "He's wearing those baggy coveralls and he's walking stooped to make us think he's old, and he's keeping his head ducked so we can't get a good look at him. But it has to be him, and I'll bet he's got Morgan in that cart. Why else would he go into the elevator? There aren't any trash cans there."

"Maybe he was taking the trash up to a Dumpster," Gus said.

"Run the video forward," Luke ordered.

They watched and, after ten minutes, the elevator doors opened and the janitor emerged, pushing the trash cart. Keeping his head down, he crossed to the closet. He came out seconds later and stuck the out-of-service sign on the elevator door, then shuffled away.

"Mark the time, then give me the camera on the elevator up top, in the plaza," Luke said.

Gus scrolled through files on the computer until he came to the right one. "Here we go. Nine thirty-eight," he said.

The three of them leaned close to study the image on the screen. For five minutes they watched as little on the screen changed.

"He never took the elevator up," Travis said, breaking the silence.

"No. He left Morgan in there, I'm sure of it," Luke said. The image of her, trapped in that elevator all these hours, made his chest constrict. Only years of training prevented him from rushing to pull her out right away.

"Later today, probably not long after the first racers arrive, he'll send the elevator up top and detonate the bomb," Travis said.

"Except we're blocking cell phone signals, so he won't be able to detonate," Gus said.

"We have to get Morgan out of there before then," Luke said.

"We can't take a chance he's got the elevator wired to blow if someone tampers with it," Blessing said.

"Can't we get some explosives guys down there to figure that out?" Luke asked.

"Maybe." Blessing looked grim. "And then we miss our best chance to get this guy—and maybe to get all the people who are helping him, too."

Luke stared at him. "So what are you saying? We wait for her to die?"

"We let him make the first move and send the elevator up," Blessing said. "He chose that elevator on purpose—not just because it's close to the action, but because it's glass. It's like Mr. Westfield said—he wants people to see what he's doing. A pretty woman with a bomb wired to her is the kind of image they'll reprint in every paper in the country and show on every television station. He'll make sure everyone has enough time to get a good look. That's when we make our move."

"I don't like it, letting him call the shots," Luke said.

"Maybe we can find a way to throw off his timing," Travis said.

"How do we do that?" Blessing asked.

Luke looked to Travis, then Gus. Like him, they appeared to be fresh out of ideas.

"He thinks the racers will start to arrive about two forty-five," Scott said. "It's what I told him, and what the papers say, too. He'll want to wait until everyone is busy celebrating the victory before he brings up the elevator."

Blessing nodded. "Go on. How do we use that to our advantage?"

Scott licked his lips, and shifted from foot to foot. "We could come in earlier, before the real competitors arrive," he said. "Maybe one forty-five. Make him think the race is ending sooner. Throw off his timing. I could pose as a racer. Dress me up like the leader, with the yellow jersey. Put some agents on bikes as racers and we can get right up to the elevator, before the real winners come along. When he raises the elevator, the agents can move in."

Blessing was shaking his head before Scott finished speaking. "We can't involve a civilian," he said.

Scott met the commander's fierce gaze, his jaw set in a stubborn line. "You're the civilians to the racing world," he said. "I was one of them. I know the route, I know how to ride and I know how to make the victory look real."

"Danny knows you," Luke said. "Won't he spot the trick?"

"Most people aren't like you," Scott said. "They don't really remember people they don't know well. And he knows Scott the crazy dishwasher. He doesn't know me as a racer. He won't expect it. Besides, he's not a fan, even though he pretended to be. He doesn't care about the athletes. To him they're just a bunch of skinny guys in spandex, helmets and goggles. If we come in before he's expecting us, we'll force him to send the elevator up early. Agents will be right there to get in."

Blessing rubbed his chin, then nodded. "All right. We'll go with your plan. We don't have time to execute anything better. I assume you'll need bicycles and uniforms?"

"I've got a friend here in town with a bike shop," Scott said. "He'll help us out. And the UCI can supply official gear."

"What about the real racers?" Travis asked.

"We'll set up a checkpoint a couple of miles away to hold them off until we've cleared the area. Gus, you take care of that," Blessing said. He turned to Travis. "Get with the Denver Police. Tell them we'll need a SWAT team to come in on light rail. We'll position the cars on the tracks nearest the plaza and they can deploy from there when we give the signal. Luke, you go with Mr. Westfield to make the arrangements for the equipment he needs."

"What about Morgan?" Scott asked.

"She'll have to wait a little longer, but we'll get her out of there as soon as it's safe to do so," Blessing said.

Chapter Seventeen

Morgan didn't know when her fear gave way to numbing calm. At some point in those hours of darkness inside the elevator she'd sunk into a kind of stupor. Maybe she was in shock, or simply exhausted and dehydrated. Her thoughts drifted to scenes of her life with her parents and Scott, then settled on replaying the time she'd spent with Luke. He was looking for her now. She was as sure of that as she was certain of her own name. The knowledge gave her strength. As impossible as her situation seemed, she wasn't going to give up hope. Danny thought he held all the cards, but she had Luke and his team fighting for her. She had to keep fighting, too. Right up until the very end.

She knew when morning came because of the increased sounds of activity overhead. She imagined the crowds gathering, the news trucks staging. Where was Danny? Was he watching it all from one of the expensive hotel rooms overlooking the plaza? Was he listening to race coverage and preparing to make his move?

More time passed and then, without warning, the elevator lurched and began to rise. Heart pounding, she looked up as the car emerged into the plaza. The sunlight blinded her, so that she had to view the scene through eyes closed to slits. She had an impression of crowds of people, of movement and bright colors.

As her eyes adjusted to the brightness, she could make out a group of riders beside the podium. One of them looked so much like Scott she knew she must be hallucinating. He wore the yellow jersey of a winner and looked so fit and confident, just as he used to.

A booming voice on a loudspeaker, audible even through the thick glass, ordered people to move away. A woman screamed, and, desperate to be free, Morgan strained against the handcuffs that bound her to the railing.

Then the elevator doors slid open and she stared across the now-vacant plaza. A row of helmeted men with heavy shields stood facing her, a hundred yards or more away. Then a single figure stepped out in front of them.

Luke, dressed in black, with a helmet and tactical vest, started walking toward her. As he drew closer, he lifted the visor on his helmet and his eyes locked to hers. The pain of the previous hours receded in the warmth of his gaze. Despite the bonds that still held her, she felt strong and safe again.

"Stop! Don't go any closer!"

The voice, loud and echoing against the stone

and glass of the surrounding buildings, froze Luke in midstride. Morgan turned her head toward the sound as Danny stepped out from behind a concrete barricade, a scoped rifle braced against his shoulder. "One shot and I'll detonate that bomb," he said, continuing to move closer. "Even if you shoot me, you won't kill me before I've destroyed you and everyone around you."

Luke faced Danny, arms held out at his sides. "Is your life really worth this?" he shouted.

"It is to make people see that these dopers and frauds are a big part of what's wrong with our world today." He gestured toward the empty podium and grandstand. "People celebrate their lies and ignore the real wrongs."

"Blowing them up won't change anything," Luke said.

"You're wrong." Danny settled the rifle more firmly against his shoulder and lowered his head to peer through the sight.

Morgan stared, as if encased in ice, unable to move, to scream, to prepare herself for the death her brain told her was coming. Time seemed frozen, too, and then with a jolt, everything unstuck, events happening so fast they were a blur of movement and color and noise.

A slim figure in a yellow jersey raced toward the shooter. "No!" Scott shouted, and launched himself at the man.

Danny turned toward her brother and in that moment Luke drew his gun and fired. The first shot caught Danny in the shoulder. The second hit him in the head. He let go of the rifle and dropped to his knees. Scott stood over him, panting, and then the SWAT team rushed in and surrounded them both, obscuring them from view.

Luke holstered his gun and ran to her. He embraced her, holding her up, and gently removed the gag from her mouth. "I knew you'd come," she said, as he cradled her face and kissed her.

"I love you." He looked into her eyes. "I wasn't about to let you go when I'd finally found you."

"You don't ever have to let me go again."

"Sir. We need you to move back now." A helmeted man with a backpack in one hand and a pair of bolt cutters in the other moved in beside them. "We've still got work to do."

Reluctantly, Luke released her. "I'll go check on Scott," he said. "But I'll be back. I promise."

"I know," she said. "You're a man who keeps his promises." The kind of man she could trust with her life—and her heart.

TWO DAYS AFTER what the newspaper dubbed the end of the Bicycle Bomber, Morgan stood before a gathering of press, city officials and law enforcement and read from a prepared statement. "I'm very grateful to the law enforcement personnel who worked tirelessly to rescue me and stop a tragedy." She looked up from her notes to find Luke in the crowd.

When he grinned at her, she couldn't keep back a smile of her own. Since her rescue, they'd been inseparable.

Had it really been only two days since that horrible ordeal? So much had happened since then. In the midst of almost unrelenting attention from the media, she'd been offered a staff job with a Colorado biking magazine. Best of all, Scott and she were growing close again. The new medication he was on was doing a good job of controlling his symptoms. But more than the medicines, the ordeal had summoned up a new strength and determination within him. The man who had launched himself at a madman in order to save her wasn't the tormented, rebellious man who had hidden from her for almost a year.

She turned and squeezed his shoulder before yielding the microphone to him. He cleared his throat and looked out at the crowd. "Some people have called me a hero for what I did," he said. "But the real heroes are the men and women in uniform who serve and protect the rest of us every day. I was simply a big brother who wanted to save his sister."

He paused for applause and cheers from the crowd, then looked back down at the paper he clutched. "I want to thank the mayor and city council for recognizing me with their service award. I also want to thank the other people and organizations who have reached out to me. I hope that I have helped others see that having a mental illness does not automatically make a person bad, or prevent him from being a contributing member of society."

He stepped back from the podium, only to be surrounded by the friends from his biking days who had rallied around him in the past forty-eight hours. He had been offered a coaching position, work as a trainer and even a book contract to write his story.

As the press conference ended, Luke found

Morgan in the crowd and pulled her aside. "You looked beautiful up there," he said.

"I'm glad it's over," she said. "I'm ready to go back to being an anonymous journalist."

"I guess the new magazine job will keep you here in Denver," he said.

"As long as I stay in Colorado, I'm good. Scott is going to be here in Denver."

"Oh? What are his plans?"

"He's decided to take a job with the bicycle shop that supplied the gear for your agents in the race. The work will be enjoyable but low stress, and he'll be close to his new doctors."

"That's good." He glanced toward where her brother stood, talking with his bicycling friends. "I'm glad he's doing so well."

"What about you?" she asked. "What are your plans?" She held her breath, waiting for the answer to that question.

"I got my new assignment this morning. Looks like I'm headed to Durango."

"Searching for the people who helped Danny?" In their time together since the bombing attempt, she'd learned a lot more about his work.

"Yes. Taking out Danny may have slowed them down, but I doubt it will stop them for long."

"Maybe I can find a way to visit," she said. "I know it's tough for you to get time off while you're on a case."

He took both her hands in his, his expression tender. "I was hoping I could persuade you to come with me."

Did he mean for a visit or something more permanent? "What, exactly, are you asking?"

"I meant it when I said I have no intention of losing you again." He pulled her close. "We have something special between us. You know that, don't you?"

"Yes." From the moment they'd met, they'd shared a connection and the events of the past week had only drawn them closer together.

"Then let's make it official," he said. "I'm okay with a long engagement, if you need that, but I want you to be my wife."

"This is crazy," she said, laughing.

"Is that a yes?"

"Yes." Before the bomber had kidnapped her, she would have said it was too soon to make such a commitment—that she and Luke didn't know each other well enough. But facing death head-on had made her realize how fragile and unpredictable life could be. Luke had risked everything for her. She could take a few risks to be with him. To love him forever.

* * * * *

MILLS & BOON®

Why shop at millsandboon.co.uk?

Each year, thousands of romance readers find their perfect read at millsandboon.co.uk. That's because we're passionate about bringing you the very best romantic fiction. Here are some of the advantages of shopping at www.millsandboon.co.uk:

* **Get new books first**—you'll be able to buy your favourite books one month before they hit the shops

* **Get exclusive discounts**—you'll also be able to buy our specially created monthly collections, with up to 50% off the RRP

* **Find your favourite authors**—latest news, interviews and new releases for all your favourite authors and series on our website, plus ideas for what to try next

* **Join in**—once you've bought your favourite books, don't forget to register with us to rate, review and join in the discussions

Visit **www.millsandboon.co.uk**
for all this and more today!